DE

AMERICAN STREET KINGS
BOOK #3

By
Bella J

ACKNOWLEDGMENTS

Editor: Lori Whitwam

Cover Design by Clarise Tan, CT Cover Creations

AUTHOR'S NOTE:

Deranged is the 3ʳᵈ book in the American Street Kings series. To fully enjoy the ride you need to read the novels in order:

DEPRAVED (Book 1)
DEFIANT (Book 2)

Deranged is a dark MC novel slapped with trigger warnings and contains scenes that will *(not might)* offend sensitive readers.

For all the dark romance readers...
ENJOY THE RIDE!
xoxo

1

ONYX

THIS WAS one of those moments when you saw everyone's lips moving, but you couldn't hear a sound. You didn't hear a single word that came out of their mouths. I sat there watching them, everyone speaking at once while trying to get their opinion heard. Dutch was practically standing on the fucking table, attempting to talk some sense into Granite.

I rubbed my palm against my beard, pursing my lips before smiling half-heartedly. "Listen, all of you can shut up now." I leaned forward, placing my elbows on the hardwood table. "I'm not taking Granite's place. I don't give a fuck who says what."

Granite shifted in his seat, turning to face me. "It's the only way."

"No, it's not."

"If we want to take down Slither and make him pay for what he's done, we need to do this."

"You are the president of the Kings, Granite. And we're not about to let you step down simply because you gave some psychopath your word."

"I agree with Onyx," Dutch chimed in. "I get why you're so hellbent on keeping to your word, but the fact that they nearly killed Neon, kidnapped Alyx, and used Tanit to do it, I say fuck 'em. It gives you more than enough right to break the deal."

Sitting next to Granite, I could hear the scratchy sound of his hand slowly rubbing down his beard. The man's brain was working overtime as he listened to the guys bicker back and forth. But it was all a waste of time. There was no way I would do this.

I glanced at Manic to my left as he watched the show with a frown on his scarred face. He looked at me and shrugged like he found the entire conversation boring as hell.

"Onyx," Granite leaned forward, "why don't you want to do this? Why don't you want to be president?"

"Because that seat right there is yours. Not mine. And I don't get why we need to fuck with how things stand around here just because of that stupid deal. Like Dutch said, they used Tanit to kidnap Alyx. If they didn't kidnap Alyx, you never would have made that deal. It's fucking entrapment, if you ask me."

Manic smirked and reached for his beer. The man never had much to say when we had our meetings. He was game for anything and didn't really care about formalities. Manic was the strong, silent type. But I knew all too well what kind of demons roamed under that marred skin.

"It's the only way." Granite lit a cigarette and blew out a cloud of smoke. "Even if my deal with Slither wasn't an issue, this is a move they won't expect. It will throw them off, momentarily letting their guard down."

"And what then? What's the plan? I become president, and we do what? Just ride over and kill 'em all?"

Ink snorted. "That sounds like the perfect plan."

"Be serious, Ink."

"I am. I'm dead fucking serious." He put out his cigarette, looking at me then at Granite. "This club is my life. You guys know that. But understand this. I don't give a fuck which one of you sits in that motherfucking chair. I am killing Slither. I am going to slice that piece of shit from nose to navel and watch him choke on his own fucking balls. That's a fact." He got up, the chair screeching across the floor. "So, it doesn't matter to me what you decide, as long as I get to watch that motherfucker suffer while I slowly pull his spine from his goddamn body. But what I will say is you better make a decision fast because I ain't waiting much longer."

Ink stormed out, the slam of the door echoing through the silence. Everyone knew he wasn't kidding. Most of the time, Ink was the jokester, the one who didn't take life too seriously. But this was different. Ever since we found Neon's mutilated body on the pavement, choking on what we thought would be her last breath, he'd changed. He was no longer the man who took each day as it came. He was a man driven by revenge, a beast hungry for blood. God knew I didn't blame him.

Manic emptied his beer, slamming the can on the table. "That went well." The rest of us scowled at him, and he shot us a cocky grin. "Someone needs to keep a sense of humor around here."

"Do you not take this seriously?" Dutch glared his way.

Manic shrugged. "Of course I do. I just don't get what the fucking problem is. Granite doesn't want to break his word to a fucking psychopath piece of shit, and Onyx doesn't want to take big brother's place. So, basically, there's two options here." He shrugged. "Either Granite shoves a huge fuck-you up Slither's ass by not giving a shit about their deal, or Onyx becomes president. It's as simple as that."

I scoffed. "Unbelievable. It's not fucking simple."

"Oh, yes, it is. You're just overcomplicating it by being a dick."

"What did you call me?"

He leaned back, all cool and collected. "Come on, Onyx. Say it. You don't want to be president because you're afraid you'll fuck up and never be as good as Granite."

Manic turned his attention to Granite. "And you don't want to break the deal because you have too much to lose now that you have Alyx. If it wasn't for the ballerina, we would already be slitting Python throats by now."

He got up, grabbed his pack of cigarettes, and walked out.

Granite cursed, Dutch groaned, and I pulled my palm down my face. But what I really wanted to do was slam my fist into something.

"Onyx—"

"Stop." I glared at Granite. "I'm not taking your place. It's a stupid fucking idea, and I'm not doing it."

Since it seemed like everyone was storming out, I did the same, whether Granite dismissed the meeting or not. Everything was fucked up now, anyway. Emotions were high, and everyone had an opinion of their own. Clearly, we wouldn't be coming to a decision today, so no use in wasting time by sitting around a goddamn table going back and forth on the same fucking subject.

"Yo, Onyx."

I let out a breath and leaned my head back. "Not now, Granite. I'm way too fucking sober for this right now."

"Is Manic right?"

I spun around, my glare meeting his gaze. "I dunno,

brother. You tell me. Is the reason you're so hellbent on keeping the deal because you're trying to keep Alyx safe? You're afraid Slither will come after her?"

"Yes." He didn't hesitate for a second. "After what I've seen them do to Neon, I can't fucking sleep at night. I almost lost her once, and there are no fucking words to describe the fear I felt while Tanit had her. I'm not taking that chance, Onyx. Not with her."

"So, that's it, then? This is all just to protect her, and fuck what the rest of us think?"

Granite took a step forward, squaring his shoulders like he always did when he tried to intimidate someone. But not me. I was long past the point where his size and that icy glare made me want to cower away to a fucking corner.

"Alyx is my life now, Onyx. And so is this club. But don't make me choose, because I swear to God, I'll choose her. I will choose Alyx if I think for one second that I can no longer protect her here."

I narrowed my eyes. "Are you saying if I don't go ahead with this, you'll leave the Kings?"

"What I'm saying is I'll do everything I can to make that son of a bitch pay for what he's done. But if the time comes when I have to make a choice, I'll choose her. It will always be her."

I shook my head. "It's not my place. That is not my motherfucking seat. It's yours, and I don't understand why we have to fuck with how things work around here."

Granite crossed his arms. "Why don't you want this?"

"Because it's not right."

"Is it because of Kate?"

"What?"

Granite relaxed his shoulders, rubbing the back of his

neck. "Listen, I know you and I haven't exactly seen eye-to-eye ever since—"

"Don't, okay? That horse has been ridden to death. Stop using Kate as an excuse for everything."

"That's not what I'm doing."

I leaned against the wall. "This has nothing to do with Kate. Yeah, we had our differences, and I was pissed because she chose you over me. But that's way in the past, brother. I'm over it."

"And Alyx?"

I scowled at him. "What about Alyx?"

"You care for her."

"Stop. Stop right there."

"It's the truth. You had a connection with her."

"Listen," I pushed myself off the wall, "I am not one of those pathetic little fucks who wants everything his big brother has. I don't envy you. I don't want your fucking life. And I sure as hell don't want your woman."

Granite pulled his pack of cigarettes from his jeans pocket. "You were there for Alyx when I couldn't be. You took care of her when I couldn't."

"Because it was the right thing to do."

"And since when do you give a fuck about doing the right thing?"

I stepped up to him, looking him straight in the eye. "Ever since you no longer do."

Seconds ticked by, and I refused to back off. Granite stared at me like he was searching for answers, but he wouldn't find any. I didn't have anything to hide. Whatever was between Alyx and me was nothing but a man caring for a woman who needed it. I backed off the second Granite had the balls to do right by her, and I hadn't given it a second's thought after that.

Granite lit a cigarette, puffing out some smoke. "Think about it. We'll discuss it some more in the morning."

"There's nothing to discuss."

Granite stomped past me, and I turned, watching him walk away. Love sure had changed him. Ever since Alyx came into his life, he was no longer the man who had nothing but hate and vengeance in his heart. But I still did. I still wanted revenge for our father's murder, not to mention what they'd done to Neon. And nothing would change that. Sure as fuck not love—or any woman.

I hated what it was doing to Ink, this infatuation he had with Neon. The bloodlust was starting to control him, and it would end up clouding his judgement, letting him make stupid mistakes.

The same went for Granite. This newfound love he claimed to have with Alyx was fucking with his mind, hence the reason he came up with the stupidest fucking idea ever.

I was vice president, and my role was to take his place when we either buried him or he was no longer able to perform the president's duties. None of that was applicable to this situation, so I refused to let things change around here simply because he gave his word to an immoral motherfucker.

2

ONYX

THERE WAS nothing like the smell of onion rings, burned steak, and spilled alcohol to make some tension roll off your shoulders. The last few days had been insane, and while emotions were running high back at the club, I needed to get the fuck out of there.

I glanced around, all the unfamiliar faces going about their own business. This wasn't exactly a top-notch bar and grill, but it was the next best thing whenever I needed to get away from everything and everyone back at our place. Some days, I would rather sit here and pay for my beer than drink it alongside a few of those assholes. Especially with Ink acting like a fucking vampire lately, only wanting blood.

"Can I get you anything else?"

I looked up at the pretty waitress smiling down at me with her please-fuck-me eyes. If it was any other day, I probably would. But my thoughts were crowding my dick, hence the reason I'd be keeping it in my pants tonight. "Just a refill."

"You got it." She took my empty beer bottle, winked at me, and turned on her heel. Her short skirt bobbed up, flashing the bottom of her ass cheeks, and her long legs accentuated by the black heels she wore looked really enticing. *Maybe tomorrow night.*

I popped a fry into my mouth, more than happy to keep to myself here in the corner booth. People were buzzing, glasses were clinking, and the bell above the door kept chiming as people walked in and out. It was almost ten p.m., and the music started to become louder.

One more beer, and I would leave this joint before the party really started. Intoxicated women seduced by tequila, and drunk men strengthened with copious amounts of beer was not the kind of crowd I was looking to hang with tonight.

The pretty waitress placed a new ice-cold beer in front of me then continued to hover.

I glanced up at her just as I was about to take a bite from my burger. "What?"

She smiled, blowing a bubble with her gum before rolling it back into her mouth with her tongue. "You gonna ask me out?"

I stuffed my mouth with a big chunk of cheeseburger, thinking that would momentarily leave me occupied and unable to answer her very direct and very presumptuous question.

"So?" She batted her eyelashes, conveying her inner thoughts of sex and sin. See, I liked my women confident and in touch with their sexuality, but I didn't like tramps thinking they owned the unicorn of all pussies.

Taking a gulp of beer to wash down the burger, I wiped my mouth. "I, uh—"

"Move along, sweetheart."

I looked to the side at curvy hips filling out a pair of leather pants perfectly. I dragged my attention up her body, a poison ivy tattoo stretching along her side and disappearing under the cropped white shirt.

"This one is already taken." She looked down at me with big blue eyes before turning back to the waitress. "So, take your little skirt and go find another guy's cock to ride. 'Kay?"

I snorted, unable to suppress an entertained smile. The waitress scowled at both of us before she turned on her heel and stomped off.

I leaned back in my seat, peering up at my heroine in leather pants. "Thanks for the help, but I actually had it handled."

"Yeah, and that's why you merely sat there with a mouth full of cheeseburger." She slid into the seat across from me, and I narrowed my eyes while taking in the fine, delicate features of her face. High cheekbones, dainty nose, and enticing as fuck, thick, tempting lips.

She held out her hand over the table. "Wraith."

"What?"

"My name. It's Wraith."

I cocked a brow, hesitant but intrigued, and shook her hand lightly. "Onyx."

"Is that your real name, Onyx?"

"Is Wraith your real name?"

Her lips curved at the edges. "I don't usually disclose such personal information on a first date."

I let out a mild laugh, amused as fuck. "I don't remember asking you out on a date."

"You don't?" She feigned a look of hurt, placing her palm on her chest. "It's bad manners to hurt a girl's feelings on the first date."

My gaze dropped to her hand, her pinky and thumb touching the swell of her perfectly palm-sized tits. Her arm was covered in ink, a sleeve tattoo of different shapes and images stretching all the way from her wrist to her shoulder.

"So, why, exactly, are you sitting here with me?"

"I just told the trampy waitress you're already taken." She shrugged. "It would look odd if I didn't sit with you." She flipped a few strands of ink-black hair out of her face, the rest tied in a high ponytail, with a white bandana wrapped around her head.

"Ah. Right." I nodded, my mouth still pulled up in an amused grin, her eyes fixed on mine. "I guess I need to buy you a drink as well, you know...to make it seem legit and all."

"Hold on, cowboy. All I did was save you from that walking STD over there. This ain't a date."

"But you just said—"

"Look at that," she glanced at her wrist with no watch, "three minutes have gone by. I bet that's enough to make our trampy friend believe my little lie."

"Wait, wh—"

"See ya, Onyx." She slid out of the seat and strolled off, leaving me with nothing but the perfect view of her curvy, firm ass.

The door chimed when she walked out, and for a second I thought about going after her. God knew it had been a long time since a woman only needed three minutes to amuse me in the way she just did. But something told me she wasn't the type of woman who would appreciate being chased after.

I finished my burger and beer in peace, my thoughts swirling back and forth from Granite wanting me to take his place, to Ink, who was on the verge of declaring World War Three on the Pythons.

How did things get so fucked up so fucking fast? This was

not how shit was supposed to go down. We were supposed to avenge our dad's death, make the Pythons pay for what they did. Instead, Neon got hurt, and Alyx got kidnapped. Now our entire fucking club seemed to hang by a goddamn thread.

The feeling of amusement I had a second ago vanished, and I shoved the napkin to the side, dropped a twenty, and walked out. This place was getting too crowded, anyway.

As I stepped outside, the warm summer breeze wafting against my cheeks, I immediately glance over to my V Rod. Two men were standing next to it, laughing while trying to keep their drunken asses standing up straight.

"Yo, step away from the wheels," I yelled as I walked over. They turned around and faced me, eyes red, foreheads sweaty and creased.

"This yours?" One with a scar above his lip glared my way.

"Yeah, so back the fuck up."

"Oooh," he mocked. "A bit overprotective, there, wouldn't you say?"

I glowered at them and grabbed my lid. "Just move along."

"Or what?"

Jesus Christ. This was not the kind of shit I was in the mood for right now. "Listen, walk away, man."

"Or what?" One guy wearing a baseball cap and a dirty pair of jeans stepped right up to me, not blinking once. I didn't even try to make myself taller, bigger, more intimidating...because I already was.

"Back up before I make you," I warned. On second thought, maybe this was the exact kind of shit I was in the mood for. Maybe picking a fight and dishing out an ass-whooping was exactly what the fucking doctor ordered.

The baseball cap douche shoved me back, and in that second, that exact moment, the one thing I could always rely on kicked in.

Instinct.

I reared back. I swung. I scored. Fucker was on the pavement eating dirt within a split second. It wasn't even hard, and I didn't need to break a sweat.

There was a tap on my shoulder, and I turned around just in time to see a fist coming my way. I pulled back, balling my fist when a hand reached over scar-face's shoulder, making him turn. The second he did, I heard a loud *thwack* and saw the fucker sway to the side.

I grabbed his shoulders and pushed him into the gravel, where he stayed. It didn't take much to whoop their drunk asses.

I looked up and found Wraith hovering over the guy, shaking her fist. She smiled. "Seems like I saved your ass twice tonight."

I smirked. "Don't flatter yourself, sweetheart."

"I'm not your sweetheart."

I nodded to the bar. "There's a waitress in there who thinks you are."

The corners of her mouth curved as she picked her backpack off the ground, swinging it over her shoulders. "It was a pleasure saving your ass. Onyx."

One of the fuckers on the ground tried to get up, but I shoved my boot against his jaw, sending him back down. "Will I see you around?"

"Don't bet on it." She sashayed that curvy ass of hers to a navy Harley Softail.

I could swear to God, I almost came in my fucking pants when I watched her get on it. She clutched that piece of hard metal so damn tight between her legs, and when I heard the roar of the engine, my cock twitched.

Wraith put her helmet on, fastening it before gripping the drag bar. "Try to stay out of trouble," she said over the beautiful noise only a Harley could make.

I shot her a cocky grin. "Don't bet on it."

She pulled out onto the street, and I stood frozen and stared at her taillight as it disappeared. I shook my head and let out a laugh while making my way to my bike. The second I got on it, I contemplated going after her again. And this time, I did.

Only...I never found her.

3

ONYX

I LEANED FORWARD on my bike, crossing my arms. "One would think that the motherfucking police commissioner would know how to be punctual."

Dutch flicked his dead cigarette my way. "Since when do you know the meaning of the word punctual?"

"Since you were dumb enough to get shot." I flipped him off and gave him a sly grin.

"I really want to say 'fuck you' right now."

"Don't." Granite smiled while placing his lid in front of him. "He'll take it as a compliment."

"I love how you know me, big brother."

A black SUV stopped on the other side of the road, and we waited until the PC got out before we approached.

"Granite," he greeted with an icy tone. Seemed like daddy dearest still needed to warm up to his future son-in-law.

"Commissioner." Granite crossed his arms.

"How is my daughter?"

"She's fine."

"Is she happy?"

Granite shifted from one leg to the other. "Yeah. Seems like it."

"Good." His voice was clipped, firm.

"Is there a reason you summoned us out here in the middle of the night? You have a job we need to take care of?"

The PC looked in the other direction, his expression unreadable. "Listen, Granite. We can no longer do business."

"What?"

The commissioner pulled out a brown envelope and held it out toward Granite. "This is everything I owe you. But as of now, we part ways."

Granite righted himself, eyebrows furrowed. "Why the sudden change of heart?"

"There's too much heat on you right now. After Alyxandria's kidnapping, and this war with the Pythons, the feds have you on their radar."

"Fuck," I cursed, kicking at the asphalt.

"I'm afraid I can't risk any involvement with you right now, Granite. It's enough to have my daughter involved with you. I can't risk any more ties to the Kings. But let me say this. As far as my daughter is concerned, I'm worried."

Granite remained silent, but I saw the way his jaw clenched, nostrils flaring. I could practically feel the anger vibrate off him. "You don't have to worry about Alyx. I'll keep her safe."

"Like you kept her safe from Tanit?"

"That was different."

"How?"

Granite stepped forward. "I let my guard down last time, and I can fucking promise you it won't happen again."

Dutch moved closer, keeping his eyes etched on the PC's bodyguards. The tension was sharp, and it made me hyperaware of the gun tucked behind my back. It would take me two seconds to grab it and aim. Those fuckers would still be balling fists by the time I had bullets flying.

The slightest movement of my hand caught Granite's attention, and he shot me a warning glare before turning his attention back to the PC. "There is no place safer for Alyx than at my side. You know me well enough to know how fucking serious I am right now."

I studied the commissioner, wondering if he'd have the balls to tick Granite off even more.

"Fine." The PC sighed. "My daughter seems to care for you a lot, which is the only reason I'm respecting her decision in this. But know this, Granite. If anything happens to my daughter, I will come after you...and I'll bring the feds with me. I swear it." He straightened his suit jacket. "But as for our business arrangement, it's off the table. At least until the heat dies down. Until then, I'll do what I can to keep the feds off your ass, but I'm not doing it for you." One of his bodyguards opened the back door of the SUV. "I'm doing it for Alyx."

He held out the envelope of cash, and I grabbed it, as Granite clearly had no intention of taking it. The man was probably too busy trying to keep his shit under control. Kicking his old lady's dad's ass probably wouldn't go down well back at home.

Granite nodded, and the PC got into the SUV. All three of us stood there as they drove off, until I finally broke the silence. "I'd say that went well, wouldn't you?"

Granite stomped past me, and Dutch flicked me on the head. "Moron."

"You see," I called after Granite, "he gets it. I'm a moron and clearly incapable of being president."

Granite turned and faced me, his expression stone. "This

is exactly why you need to step the fuck up, Onyx, so we can end this war with the Pythons once and for all."

"Seriously? That is what you got from that conversation?" I moved closer. "While you were standing there doing a pretty good job at keeping your anger under control, I was imagining a hundred and one ways to kick the PC's ass. You see the dilemma, right?"

"All I'm seeing is my little brother who refuses to acknowledge his place in this club. You are the vice president. You are my successor. Surely, you knew this day would come sooner or later."

"Yeah, well, I was bargaining on later. Not fucking sooner."

Granite grabbed his lid. "Things don't always work out the way we plan, Onyx. It's time you realized that. I know me giving that piece of shit my word seems trivial to you, but I won't stoop to their level. I will not become the same immoral fucker Slither is. I made a deal. And now I have to live with that. And unfortunately, so do you."

"All of us do, man." Dutch revved his Harley, the low rumble thundering through the night. No matter who, where, or what, that fucking sound always grabbed me by the balls.

I had always known Dutch had this direct line to Granite's thoughts. I'd swear to God, Granite could give him half a glance, and the fucker would know exactly what Granite wanted him to do. And that was probably why Dutch decided to ride off without us, since Granite sent him some telepathic fucking message to give us some privacy.

I groaned, already knowing the discussion that was about to take place.

"Listen, Granite—"

"You need to do this, Onyx. We don't have a choice." He sounded grave, serious. Desperate.

"I disagree. We always have a choice, man. I told you, you don't have to keep your word to a piece of shit like Slither."

"And I told you it's not just about him."

"I know. God!" I kicked at the dirt, my pulse racing as rage burned its way through my chest. "I know you're protecting Alyx. I get that. But as much as she's your woman, this club is supposed to be your home. Your life."

"It was." Granite's expression turned somber, eyes creased at the corners. "It was until she became my life. My home. But it's also about more than that. It's about all of us. You and I, Dad left us in charge of this club because he trusted us. He trusted that we would do whatever needed to be done to protect each and every member, to give them what they deserved. And what they deserve is revenge."

I charged forward, stopping a few feet from him. "And we can give them that. Why do you have to step down for it to happen?"

He took a deep breath, craning his neck and looking up at the sky. That was one thing missing in the New York sky at night. Stars. You didn't see any since city life polluted and pretty much ruined the air around us.

"Tell me the truth." He looked at me. "Tell me the real reason you don't want to be president."

"I don't have time for this." I turned my back on him and got onto my Harley, starting the ignition before putting on my lid.

"Onyx."

The sound of the engine ripped through the night, echoing far in the distance. I bit my lip, clutching the ape-hangers tight. "I don't want to take your place because

there's not a chance in hell I'll ever be a good president." I
glanced at him. "Not like you, big brother."

There was nothing left to say, so I rode off, leaving
Granite behind. For the first time since all this fucked up
shit happened, I managed to tell the truth. Even though
every word coated my tongue with bitterness, I hoped
Granite would now leave well enough alone and just let me
be Onyx. Vice president of the American Street Kings and
brother to the president. I didn't want to be more than that. I
didn't have it in me to be more. Everyone always said I was a
loose cannon, a wildcard waiting to wreak havoc. And I
never denied it. I was all about breaking rules, not enforcing
them. Besides, if it wasn't for our dad's instructions and
dying wish for Granite to be president and me to be VP, I
never would have accepted the rank. I would have been
happy as a pig in mud with the sergeant-at-arms tag. Or any
rank that required a trigger-happy maniac like me. But the
day I accepted the VP tag, it never crossed my mind once
that I'd have to one day step up and take Granite's place. He
was so good at leading. Still was. His shoulders were broad
enough to carry the responsibility. Mine weren't. Responsibilities and I simply didn't get along.

Besides, once I got that tag on my cut, I was sure the day
Granite needed to be replaced...I'd be dead.

4

WRAITH

I'VE BEEN to many bars in my life, seen a lot of the restrooms some of them have. But I had yet to find one that had a decent sink, walls without lipstick graffiti, and toilet doors without the phrase 'John and Eve fucked here, December 21st, 2012.' With the amount some of these holes charged for a beer, one would think they could afford a better place for a person to take a piss.

My reflection in the dirty, oval-shaped mirror mocked me. I hadn't seen the real me look back at me since I was ten years old. All I saw was an unfamiliar face, and eyes with too much eyeliner and too little humanity. Benevolence had been stolen from me, and all it left behind was an empty vessel of fake smiles, phony laughs, and simulated words hidden within mundane conversations.

I glanced down at the spot on my wrist untouched by black ink. There wasn't a real reason behind my decision not to have that piece of skin tattooed. Maybe I was waiting for inspiration to hit me with an image that would seal that last void on the flesh of my right arm.

Void.

Wraith.

Perfect alias.

The restroom door swung open, the hinges creaking as two women came stumbling in, drunk on their asses. It wasn't even three p.m. on a Sunday afternoon, and already the tramps came out to play.

Their drunken laughter sent a bolt of instant annoyance to my brain. No one could ever be that fucking happy. Not even copious amounts of alcohol had the power to conjure up such ecstatic behavior. It was stupid. They were stupid.

I crouched and zipped down my mid-leg boot to secure the hidden blade. A lesson I learned a long time ago, that a woman could never be too careful. As I straightened, I gave myself a last once-over in the dirty mirror, scrunched up my ponytail, and popped my lips. The black straps of my bra showed under the gray shirt I was wearing, and the ever-increasing summer heat had forced me to wear a pair of jean shorts rather than my preferred leather pants.

The loud buzz of the bar hit me the second I walked out of the restroom, laughter and cheerfulness spreading like a fucking infection. Most of those smiles plastered on unfamiliar faces were alcohol-induced, people trying to pretend they were happy, that life was treating them well. But it wasn't. And even if life threw you a bone every now and then, you'd pay for that motherfucking bone with blood some time or another. Guaranteed. Life favored no one. Some people were just better at pretending than others.

Approaching the bar, my tequila was ready and waiting for me, the bartender standing with a huge grin on his face. "Still one on the hour, every hour?"

I took the shot glass and held it up, smiling back at him. "No lemon."

"No lemon." He placed a new beer on the counter and wiped his hands before tending to other customers.

The shot of tequila was instantly forgotten the second I swallowed. Alcohol had lost its ability to sting and burn my insides years ago. I couldn't even remember the last time I cringed after drinking a shot.

The sound of roaring engines came from outside, a rolling thunder of power vibrating through the bar. I closed my eyes, loving the echo of what some people would interpret as noise, yet I appreciated as music. There was nothing quite like it, the low rumble of a Harley engine. Put a few of them together, and you had yourself a fucking melody.

I smirked to myself when I noticed all the curious eyes stare out the windows. One would think a bar like this would be used to motorcycle crew visits on a Sunday afternoon. After all, this place was the farthest out of town with a decent menu and reasonable prices. On a sunny day like this, it was every biker's wet dream.

The doors opened, and I could hear their shit-kicker boots hit the concrete floor. Not even the eighties rock song playing on the jukebox in the corner could hide the sound.

I didn't turn around. Didn't pay them any attention. The entire bar was already making them feel like gods as they walked in.

The bartender held up a hand. "Yo, Granite. What can I get you, man?"

"The usual."

"And for the lady?"

I took a quick glance over my shoulder at the lady in question—a petite blonde who practically disappeared at the side of the mountain she was walking next to.

"Screwdriver for the lady."

The man had the kind of voice that could silence a room

with a single fucking syllable. Deep, low, husky, and intimidating as fuck. Around here, everyone knew who he was. You didn't need to see the skull and American flag patch on his cut to know he was the president of the American Street Kings. His reputation preceded him—the King who once ruled the streets of New York before the Pythons started moving in on their turf.

I turned my attention back to the beer I was nursing when I heard a familiar voice behind me. A smile tugged at the corner of my lips as I turned in my seat, staring at the man across the room. His sky-blue irises swept my way, an amused grin appearing on his face when he recognized me.

He rubbed his fingers across his beard as he sauntered closer. "You again."

I nodded. "You remember me."

"How can I forget?" He stopped a few feet away. "You were the date I didn't go on a date with."

"That makes no fucking sense."

"And neither did our date."

For a small eternity, I held his gaze, those pretty blues of his not even blinking. I'd be a fool not to have noticed how dangerously attractive he was with his dirty blond hair all disheveled, and unruly beard all manly and buff. Not to mention those broad shoulders and six-foot-three of pure muscle and testosterone. It would be hard to miss a man like him—especially with those pretty 'fuck-me' eyes.

He grabbed a beer from the waiter and stepped in next to me. "What's a girl like you doing in a place like this all on her own?"

"What makes you think I'm on my own?"

He shrugged. "No man in his right fucking mind will leave a woman like you alone and unattended in a bar like this."

"Oh, my God." I rolled my eyes. "Does that line even work?"

"Sure does," he replied unabashedly.

"Well," I took a sip of my beer and swallowed, "if a girl is dumb enough to fall for that, she deserves to get played."

A low laugh rolled over his lips, a sound that demanded my attention be turned to his mouth. His lower lip was heavier, the corner of his mouth twitching. There was a visible line through his beard on the side of his chin, the remnants of what I guessed was once a scar on his face.

I glanced down at the tag on his cut. "Vice president, huh?"

"Yup."

"So, you're a King?"

He closed his eyes as a little moan rumbled in the back of his throat. "God, I love it when a woman calls me her king."

"I did not say you're my—"

"Yes, you did."

"No, I didn't."

"You did."

"Stop." My lips quirked up, unable to hide my amusement. "You're an ass."

His brows drew together. "First I'm your king, and now I'm an ass?"

"Oh, my God." I took a sip of my beer to mask the smile that was threatening to appear. The last thing this guy needed was to see that I was entertained by his egotistical humor.

"Which crew do you ride with?"

"What makes you think I ride with any crew?"

He shrugged. "With a ride like yours, you have to be."

"No." I shook my head. "I don't ride with a crew. I'm what you would call a free rider."

"I find that hard to believe."

"Well, believe it."

With his elbow on the bar, he leaned to the side, eyes studying me, and his mouth pulled up in a smirk. "So, where did you disappear to the other night?"

"I went home."

"I tried to follow you."

"You followed me?"

He lifted a shoulder. "Tried. *Tried* should be the word we're focusing on here."

"I'm sorry, I'm too busy being freaked out by the word *followed* to focus on any other words coming out of your mouth right now."

The confident smirk remained on his face, and he wasn't the least bit concerned that I'd take him for a stalker rather than a potential lay. "We were on a date. I had to make sure you got home safe."

"Yet you failed."

He shifted closer. "I can promise you it wasn't due to lack of trying."

I cocked a brow. "Onyx, is it?"

"Yup." He pretended to look around, thinking. "Um, it's something with a...wait, don't tell me." He snapped his fingers. "Poltergeist."

"Wraith."

"Same thing."

I crossed my arms. "I'm starting to regret saving you from walking around with gonorrhea right now."

His face lit up, and he laughed. "I guess I owe you one."

"Yeah, you do."

With a wave of his hand, he called the bartender over. "Let me guess. You're a tequila girl."

"What gave it away?" I stared out in front of me, not looking at him.

"I can figure out a lot of things about people solely by looking at them."

I swallowed, a sudden discomfort forcing me to clear my throat.

"Well, that, and the three empty shot glasses in front of you." He motioned to the bartender, indicating he wanted two of whatever was in the empty shot glasses.

For some unknown reason, relief settled in the pit of my stomach. The mere thought of anyone *figuring* me out wasn't exactly comforting.

I gathered my composure and relaxed a little into the seat. "That could have been any liquor."

"No. It was tequila."

"How can you tell?"

He shifted closer, his broad shoulders and tall frame boxing me in. "I observe. See, even though there are no traces of lemon, lime, or salt, by looking at you, I can tell that only the best will do." He leaned his head to the side, those blue irises scrutinizing every contour of my face. "And everyone knows tequila is best."

Oh, he was good. He was really good. And if that mastered charming act of his wasn't enough to seduce, the woody scent that wafted off him would surely do the trick.

I licked my lips, the movement catching his attention. The chair swiveled as I turned it slightly so I could come as close to him as possible, and I crossed my legs. His jaw set, lips slightly parted as his eyes met mine.

I leaned toward him, shifting in my seat so I could bring

my face closer to his. I inhaled deeply, and the vein in his neck started to throb faster.

"Your smell, it's woody. Spicy. Cumin, maybe? And there's something citrusy, something fresh and...enticing." His throat bobbed as he swallowed, and my lips twitched. I pulled back a little so I could look into his eyes. "Let me guess. Armani Code, is it?"

He pressed his lips together, his gaze not letting go of mine for even half a second. The summer heat and cigar smoke filling the bar couldn't stop the space between us from becoming palpable. Intense.

I shot him a smirk. "See, I'm good at figuring out people too. And judging by your expensive taste in cologne, it's clear only the best will do for you."

The edges of his mouth turned up, the first sight of a devilish grin. The blue hues in his irises seemed to darken as he kept staring at me. Seconds passed without us saying a word, and I could practically hear his fucking heartbeat.

The slight tap of his finger on the counter filled the silence between us, and he pursed his lips before straightening and grabbing his beer. "I'll see you around."

I tipped my beer bottle his way. "I guess you will."

With a grin on his face, he walked off, and I turned in my seat. "Onyx," I called.

"Yeah." He glanced at me.

"Next time you follow me, try to keep up." I winked, and he bit his lower lip before turning back and heading over to where the rest of his crew sat.

The guy might be an asshole, but somehow, he made assholery look good.

5

ONYX

"Who's your friend?" Manic tipped his beer toward the bar.

"Someone I met the other night."

"She's good looking."

I shot him a warning glare when I caught him ogling her. "Take those manwhore eyes of yours off her."

"She your old lady?"

"No."

"Then I'll keep my manwhore eyes on her, fuck you very much."

If I was able to slice through his skull with my eyeballs, I would have done it right that instant. Fucker might have a grotesque mark on his face, but the ladies loved him. It was like that scar was a fucking chick magnet.

"She ride with anyone?" Granite placed his arm around Alyx's shoulders.

"She says she doesn't."

"A woman as fine looking as her?" Manic chimed in. "I find that hard to believe. If she's not riding with anyone, she has to be fender-fluff."

"Do you *want* a piece of glass in your eye?"

Manic smirked all open mouthed while chewing on some peanuts, and Dutch slapped him on the head. "Stop fucking with the guy, would ya?"

I settled in my seat, throwing warning glares in Manic's direction every ten seconds. The annoying-as-fuck smirk remained on his face, making it clear his new goal for today was to piss me off.

"It's been weeks," I said to Granite. "When is Ink going to start joining the club on rides?"

"The man's a little preoccupied, with Neon's rehabilitation and all."

"That guy does not catch a clue, does he? Neon doesn't want him."

Alyx reached for her drink. "I wouldn't say that."

"What? The woman has been begging him to leave her the fuck alone for weeks now."

"Yeah, but I get the feeling it's like this inside game between them."

"Like what? He chases her like a dog with his tail between his legs, and she kicks him in the balls every time?"

Alyx chuckled. "Something like that."

"Fucking masochist, if you ask me."

Manic slammed his empty beer bottle on the table and whistled to a waitress for a refill before turning his attention back to me. "So, Onyx. You decided whether you'll be the new boss yet?"

With a snarl, I kicked my boot into his shin. "Shut the fuck up."

"What? Everyone here's thinking it. I'm just the only one with the balls to ask."

Alyx got up from her seat, shooting us a knowing smile. "I need to use the restroom."

Granite's old lady caught on quick, knowing we didn't discuss crew matters in front of women...until Manic.

"Dude, seriously?" I stared at him in disbelief.

"Onyx is right. No talking shit in front of the ladies."

Manic held his hand up in surrender. "My bad. But I'm serious, though. Onyx, what's your deal, man?"

I chugged down the rest of my beer, and the waitress came around just in time for me to place the empty bottle on her tray. "Can a guy not get drunk in peace without discussing crew shit?"

"Nope."

"You're lucky I actually like you, or I'd be wiping that smirk off your face with my fist."

Manic straightened. "Dude, look at this scar and tell me if you think that would actually get me to shut up."

Granite and Dutch laughed, and I glared holes into his forehead. But Manic ignored my stares of hell. "So? Have you decided?"

"I have. But it doesn't seem like anyone wants to accept my answer."

Granite placed his arms on the table. "As long as the answer is no, it will be ignored, yes."

I scoffed. "And they call this a free country."

"Listen, Onyx," Granite started with his *time-to-get-serious* voice, "we need to work on a plan to get this crew where it was before Slither fucked with us. And we can't do that until this final decision has been made."

I refused to look at him, rather staring at the label on my beer bottle, which I was slowly pulling off at the edges. "I know," I replied, clipped. Even though taking Granite's place was the last fucking thing I wanted to do, I wasn't an idiot. I knew we were running out of time, and some of us were running out of patience. "I still think it's bullshit that you need to keep up your part of the deal."

Granite shrugged as he sat back. "What is a man if his word ain't solid?"

"I'll tell you what he's not. Stupid."

Manic laughed. "That's a good one."

"Shut up," Granite and I said in unison, and the guy actually seemed offended for a second.

"Fine," he got up and grabbed his beer, "I'll go keep the pretty lady over there company. She looks like she could appreciate a big old scar."

I jumped up and glowered at him. "Are you serious right now?"

Dutch held a palm in front of his face as he snickered, and Manic smiled, slapping his hands on my shoulders. "Dude, chill. I promise I won't break her...much."

Everyone erupted in laughter while I was the only one about to have an aneurysm.

"The guy's fucking with you, little brother."

I turned and saw Manic leaning on the bar beside Wraith, smiling like a fucking male stripper with super white teeth. "Do you see that?" I looked at Granite, but my brother just kept laughing.

I pursed my lips, biting the inside of my cheek as I took my seat. "I guess the joke's on me today, is it?"

Dutch slapped me on the shoulder. "It sure is."

"Ha, fucking ha. I ain't coming on these runs until Ink drags his ass with us. At least then you'll be picking at his ass and not mine."

Everyone continued to laugh, and I glanced over my shoulder at Wraith. Manic shot me a coy smile, going the extra distance to piss on my goddamn battery. God, you had to love these fuckers.

"I'm gonna go get us a round of bourbon," Granite said as he got up and sauntered to the bar.

I ran a hand through my hair and let out a breath. "God, this is bullshit."

Dutch lit a cigarette. "Listen, man, I get why you're doubting. Granite has big boots to fill, and you're afraid you won't be able to man up. But you need to give yourself some credit. Both of you have Stone's blood running through your veins."

"I'm not like my brother."

"And you don't have to be. You don't have to be Granite to be a good president, Onyx."

I pulled a palm down my face, feeling like I had the fucking world on my shoulders. "You don't get it. No one gets it. I'm the irresponsible one. The one who needs a fucking leash. Put me in that motherfucking chair, then who's gonna keep me in check?"

Dutch stared at me with a half-smile on his face. "You are."

"What?"

He tapped his finger against the cold beer in front of him. "I get it. It's easier to ignore the rules than it is to enforce them. Right now, you have your brother to worry about your actions. But if you're president, you'll no longer have that luxury."

I pulled my mouth in a hard line, and Dutch smirked. "Besides thinking you won't be able to fill Granite's shoes, you're afraid to grow up."

"What the fuck is that supposed to mean?"

"It means the day you got the VP tag, you made an oath to this club to step in as leader when we needed you to. And right now, we need you to, Onyx. Granite needs you to. Do not think for one second this is easy for your brother, to step down. But he's doing what needs to be done for everyone he cares about. Now you gotta do the same."

I shook my head, pursing my lips. "This is not how it was supposed to be."

"Nothing ever is. Nothing ever works out the way we planned. All I'm saying, Granite has Alyx now. The Kings have this war with the Pythons. Don't make Granite choose between this club and the woman he loves, because he won't choose us, I can promise you that."

"I know." I clutched my fists in front of my mouth. "I fucking know that."

Dutch leaned forward, eyes boring into mine. "Then grow the fuck up and do the right thing."

Alyx returned just as Granite placed a tray of bourbon shots on the table. He wrapped an arm around her waist, pulling her closer and kissing her like they weren't standing in a bar surrounded by a fuck-load of people.

I cleared my throat. "Ahem...put your dick back in your pants, please."

"Why?" Granite looked over my shoulder toward the bar. "Manic seems to have his out."

"Oh, my God," I muttered. "I'm gonna kick all your asses."

6

ONYX

THE DAY I accepted the VP tag, I didn't think it would ever come to this. I had always been so sure I'd take my last breath long before my brother did. But I never could have predicted things would work out the way they did. For the first time, I was forced to think about how it would be to lead this crew. How it would be to sit in the president's chair and hold the future of the Kings in my hands. It wasn't a responsibility I ever thought would be mine.

I sat behind the wheel of the black cage. Whenever we had this kind of meeting, we made sure we pitched with four wheels. It was easier to get away if shit should hit the fan.

Ink was sitting in the passenger seat, with Granite, Dutch, and Manic in the back.

The sun had started to set on the horizon, but the pretty pinks and yellows did nothing to lessen the dark foreboding I felt in my bones.

"Something doesn't feel right." I tapped my finger against the wheel.

Ink stared out the window. "Yeah, I feel ya. But we have no choice. We need the business."

"Yo, Granite," I called to the back. "What time did they say they'd be here?"

"Seven."

I glanced at the clock on the dash. Ten past seven. I searched the area, but there was no sign of them. "Something's not right. They're never late."

My leg started to twitch, juddering up and down to the same rhythm my finger continued to tap on the wheel. The prickle of warning I felt a few seconds ago was making its way to the center of my stomach.

"Granite—"

"Let's give them five more minutes."

"In the last ten years, they have been punctual as fuck. I'm telling you, man, something ain't right."

"Five more minutes, Onyx."

I mumbled under my breath, swiping my fingers across my beard. I became increasingly aware of the gun at my side and the blade in my boot. Ink was packing; I knew that for sure. He never left the compound without at least two guns and a knife.

Abruptly, Ink sat up straight. "You hear that?"

I tilted my head to the side, listening.

"Harleys?"

"Yup, those are definitely hogs."

Ink looked at me, his face red with warning. "Since when do the Sixes roll with hogs?"

My heart raced. "Since never. Granite, we got company, and it's safe to say it ain't good."

"I hear it." Granite, Dutch, and Manic were out the back door before I could even open mine.

Ink launched out, gun in hand and slowly walking in the direction from where the hogs were coming.

As I rounded the cage, I saw the Harleys appear in the distance. They were slowly coming toward us, and I already knew it was them. The Pythons. I could feel it in my blood, the way it singed the inside of my veins. It was the same feeling I got the night my father died. It was an ominous feeling that ignited a certain caveat that had my every instinct flared and prepared for onslaught. Unfortunately, that night, the second I saw my father go down, every instinct I had to kill and maim turned into a compulsion to protect and save. But I couldn't protect him. I couldn't save him.

None of us could.

"It's the Pythons," Ink said with a low sneer, yet sounding oddly excited about it.

"Everyone, stay cool." Granite held up his hand, cautioning us.

My heart started to pound inside my chest, adrenaline washing through every nerve ending. Even my fingers became itchy, the gun at my side screaming to be pointed at a fucking Python.. Slither might think he had the Kings by the balls, but I wouldn't think twice about putting a bullet in his skull right after I carved his heart out and fed it to the fucking rats.

From the corner of my eye, I noticed Ink's fists clench at his sides. Anger vibrated off him in waves. Toxic. Deadly. Every empath's motherfucking nightmare.

Dutch slid in next to Ink, while Granite moved to the front. Manic was standing at my right, a huge smile on his face. I could swear to God, the day World War Three should break out, this man would be manically and ecstatically fucking happy. *Psycho.*

There were about six or seven hogs coming our way, cruising toward us like arrogant assholes, as if they owned the fucking world. The loud thunder of their engines rumbled, slamming against the concrete slabs holding the bridge above us.

Manic loosened his shoulders, leaning his head from side to side. "I knew my spidey senses were tingling."

I glowered at him. "What the fuck, man?"

"What?"

"You need to lay off the fucking superhero movies. Seriously."

"Would you two shut up?" Ink scolded, and the tattoos on the side of his face seemed even creepier than the scar on Manic's.

I stood a step behind Granite, arms crossed in front of my chest. I was about the only guy who matched Granite in length. We got our over six feet size from our dad. Big, butch, and brutal.

The fleet of Pythons came to a stop, revving their engines in a bid to add some good measure of intimidation. But they didn't intimidate us. They only enticed us with the prospects of painting the asphalt with the blood seeping from their broken skulls.

Slither was first to take off his lid, slowly getting off his bike. "Well, well, well." He inhaled deeply, shoulders rising as he took in the long breath of air.

Melodramatic asshole.

"Do I smell betrayal?" His freaky as fuck eyes cut straight to Granite, and I tensed, ready to do some target practice on his fucking forehead. Granite remained stoic, and Slither sauntered closer with his tribe of snakes close behind. "I thought we had a deal."

"We do," Granite replied, clipped.

Slither *tsk'd*. "Do you take me for a fool?"

"A fool, no." I glared at him. "An ugly motherfucker, yes."

Slither shot me a sideways glance, his expression taunting me with blatant disinterest. Granite was the one he wanted to crack, not me. With a simple look my way, he made it clear he didn't deem me a threat, not like he did Granite. Big mistake.

"You should get a leash on your little brother, Granite." Slither pulled his palm over his clean-shaved head. "Before it gets infected and goes rabid."

It was instinct. It overwrote every logical thought, and I reacted by wanting to launch forward, already envisioning my hands coated with the fucker's blood. But Granite reached out, slamming an arm in my chest, cutting me off and stopping me from attacking. I hissed and glared at Slither. "The day will come when I bathe in your fucking blood, I swear it."

Slither's brows almost touched his hairline, his palm placed on his chest. "Such aggression. It's hurting my feelings."

"When I'm done with you, it will be much more than just your feelings hurting." The threat hung between us, thick and toxic, and I wanted it to explode. I wanted it to take control of us so we could end this once and for all. "You sure have a big mouth when all of us here have at least one reason for wanting to slice your throat."

Slither laughed, and his legion of delinquents joined in. He pulled out a cigarette and lit it, the smell of nicotine and deadly tension wafting over us.

The cloud of smoke he blew out drifted away in the breeze, and I stood there hoping he would choke on his next goddamn breath.

"I thought we had a deal." He looked straight at Granite.

"I tell you where your girl is, and you stay out of my fucking business. Was that not our deal?"

"It was." Granite finally removed his arm from my chest, stepping closer to Slither. "We have a deal."

"Then why go behind my back, setting up a meeting with *my* buyers?"

"Buyers you stole from us by enforcing a deal that, in my opinion, means nothing," I spat. "This fucking deal you're referring to would never have happened if you didn't kidnap Alyx in the first place." I was ready to rip his fucking head off, practically smelling the stench of his rotting corpse. There was no word in the dictionary that could aptly relay the magnitude of my hate toward this motherfucking demon.

Slither shrugged. "What can I say? My plan was brilliant."

"Your plan will soon bite you in the ass."

"Is that a threat?"

"Sure is."

He smiled, his split tongue darting out of his mouth, the tentacles twisting and curving like devil fingers. "Oh, I doubt you'll ever have the balls to make good on that threat...*little brother*."

More than anything, I wanted to wipe that mocking look from his face by peeling his skin off, one tattooed snake scale at a time.

He turned his attention to Granite. "But maybe the little brother will do better at keeping his word."

"Fuck off, Slither," Granite snarled. "You're not exactly the one who can take the moral high ground around here."

"True." He flicked his cigarette butt a few feet away. "But I'm not you." He lurked closer, menace oozing out of him like pus, his existence as vile as a septic wound. "I'm not the notorious Granite, president of the American Street Kings. The man known for his underhanded deal- ings with the rich and his noble acts toward the poor. You have a reputation to uphold, people to impress. Me? I don't give a fuck what people think about me. And the best part? I don't have to give a fuck because no one expects me to be," he licked his lips, "a man of my word...like you."

Dutch moved closer, Ink and Manic now flanking us. Everyone's instinct was on high alert, my senses tuned in to every threat. Hate and rage pulsed between us and them like the heartbeat of hell. We were on the brink of cold-blooded carnage, and I desperately wanted to be tipped over that edge so I could unleash the bloodlust that seethed inside me.

Granite stood strong, the epitome of cool, calm, and collected. It was something he did well, pretending to be unfazed and settled in extreme circumstances. But I knew all too well what kind of turbulence stormed under that cool façade. Granite was two seconds away from ripping Slither's tongue out.

Slither cocked his head, never taking his eyes off Gran- ite. "What's the matter, big man? Cat caught your tongue?" His split tongue slithered out of his mouth, moving around like insect feelers in the fucking wind.

Granite took an intimidating step forward, close enough for Slither to drive a blade in his abdomen if he wanted to. But Granite held the tension, like a pebble in the palm of his hand, controlling where it would land next.

"You might think you have the upper hand, Slither. That you're one step ahead of us. But that ill-placed confidence of yours will be your downfall."

"Listen to that. Two threats in one day." Slither grinned,

amusement sticking to his face like dirt. "Must be my lucky day."

"You bet your ass it is," Ink interrupted. "If it wasn't, I'd be standing with your spine in my hand right about now."

Slither looked his way. "Such hatred." He closed his eyes and let out a moan. "Hmmm. It's giving me a hard-on."

"Fuck you," Ink spat, his entire body shaking.

"I know you have more than enough reason to want my head on a spike." He shrugged. "After all, I did ruin one of your own. Or was it two?" He feigned a thoughtful look. "Well, three if you count the girl with the unicorn pussy. What's her name again? Magenta? No. Indigo—"

"Neon, you sick fuck!" Ink's words practically bled out of his mouth.

"Oh, yes." He pinned his stare on Ink. "Neon."

"I'm going to gut you, I swear to God."

Slither smirked, his men moving closer. "You know, some nights when I can't sleep, I can still hear her screams. Her pleas. The way she begged for us to stop. I'll tell you, I've never enjoyed jerking off as much as I do when I think of her blood coating my cock."

Ink roared, and by the time Dutch and I reacted, it was too late. Ink launched at Slither, a balled fist in the air, and then the crack of bone against bone.

Chaos erupted, the sounds of grunts and curses becoming the prelude of guaranteed carnage. Ink's face was that of pure hatred, rage, an all-consuming frenzy of a need to spill blood. The man was unstoppable as he hit Slither one punch after the other, a scream ripping from his throat.

While Dutch tried to pull Ink off Slither, I reached for my gun, placing my finger on the trigger. But there was no way I'd be able to aim and shoot without risking one of our guys. Not even I was that good a shot.

Granite tried to reach for Ink, but some motherfucker came from the side and went straight for him. With my gun in hand, I reacted and launched forward, planting the back of my gun right in the guy's face, and he stumbled back.

Two more men rushed toward us, but I was ready and ducked when one of them swung his fist, aiming for my face. As I came back up, I knocked the fucker out by connecting my fist with his jaw from below, his neck craning back as he fell.

Everything was happening so damn fast, there was no time to think. Taking a split second to breathe, I turned just in time to see Slither punch Ink in the gut, followed by an uppercut to the jaw. Blood was already pissing from his nose, the sides of his mouth.

Suddenly, all I heard was my own heartbeat, flashbacks of the night my father died piercing through my mind like poisonous darts. For a split second, I was transported to that moment—the moment my dad fell to the ground, blood pooling around him.

I'd seen men die before, but nothing I'd ever witnessed came close to that image, witnessing the life drain from my father's body. Watching someone I cared about, someone I loved, take his last breath. The pain smothered the bloodlust. The heartache crucified the hate I felt for the Pythons. All that mattered right then was that I would lose my dad. And as he closed his eyes for the last time, I vowed vengeance and swore I would never allow anyone else I cared about die at the hands of the fucking Pythons.

That was a promise I intended to keep.

I lifted my hand, placed my finger on the trigger, and the gunshot cracked through the air. The echo of the shot was replaced with utter and complete silence, all the men who tried to kill each other mere moments ago frozen and silent.

I clenched my jaw, biting my tongue as I glared from one face to the other. "The day will come when we kill each other, but today is not that day."

"Fuck that." Ink spat out a mouthful of blood. "I'm ready to massacre these motherfucking reptiles, right here, right now," he yelled.

Slither snarled, his split tongue grazing against his top teeth. "Bring it."

"No!" Granite snapped then stepped in next to me, a smear of blood painted across his eyebrow. "Onyx is right. This is not the time or the place. Cops will be here any second."

Slither grunted before spitting on the ground. "Your man started it." He shot Ink a warning glare, and Ink growled at him like a starved animal. "Seems like your SAA here has a soft spot for the pixie."

"Don't you fucking talk about her," Ink warned, yanking forward, but Manic jumped in front of him, keeping him back.

"Everyone calm the fuck down," Granite's voice boomed through the night.

I walked over to Ink and grabbed his elbow, pulling him close. "Calm down, man," I muttered with my back turned to the Pythons. "I know how much you want this, but when it comes to revenge, timing is everything. And today. Is not. That. Time. Feel me?"

Ink still bared his teeth, never taking his eyes off the man he hated the most. I could practically feel the flames of hell burning through his flesh. "Go back to the cage and calm down."

I let go of Ink's arm, and Dutch gave me a knowing nod. Ink stepped to the side, his stare of death never leaving Slither. "One day, man. One day I will make you look me in the eye while I carve out your goddamn spleen."

Slither smirked. "I can't wait."

The wild look in Ink's eyes screamed all sorts of crazy. The man was shaking, sheer adrenaline fueling his anger and need to make Slither pay for what they did to Neon. I didn't blame him. We all felt that way. But today was not that day, no matter how much we wished it was.

Slither wiped at the blood in the corner of his mouth, snorting when he saw the crimson smear on the top of his hand. "How is she doing, by the way? The pixie girl with the screams of an angel?"

"Don't," I warned, lifting my gun and aiming at his head. In an instant, Granite and I had six other guns in our faces.

Time stood still. No one even breathed as death hung over us like the veil of hell. If I had to pull the trigger, Slither would be dead by the time his crew got to shooting us. It would be worth it, though, that split second of watching my bullet cracking his skull wide open. If it was just me, I'd do it. But Granite was here too, and no matter how much I wanted to see Slither dead, his existence erased from this world, my need to protect my brother was stronger.

I tightened my jaw, taking one more second to imagine what it would feel like to kill him, before I lowered my gun.

Slither's face pulled up as he smiled. "Seems like I've underestimated you, Onyx. Here I thought your older brother was the only one with balls in your crew."

"Shut up, Slither." Granite stepped up, his presence as heavy as a goddamn wrecking ball. "Like my brother said, the day will come when this war ends between us. But it's not today."

Slither's freaky-ass eyes cut to Granite. "Remember our deal, good man. Don't fuck with my business."

"What? Like you fucked with ours?" I chimed in, but Slither ignored me and continued to keep Granite's stare.

"That ballerina girl of yours is safe back at the compound because of me."

"Talk about her again, and I'll cut out that mother-fucking tongue of yours." Granite stepped up, and I was sure he got taller within two seconds.

Slither licked his lips, the two tentacles of his tongue slipping in and out of his mouth. "Just remember how easy it was for me to get to not only one, but three of your women. I could do it again." He lifted a shoulder. "That's if you don't keep to your end of the bargain."

I stepped up, halfway forcing myself between Granite and him. "Let's go."

Granite's jaw ticked, his eyes dark orbs of malice. He was frozen to the spot, and it cost me a slight nudge against his chest to get him moving.

"Make no mistake, Slither," I started as I continued to walk back, "you're on borrowed time."

He smirked, the evil he reeked of spreading for miles.

Dutch pulled up behind us, and I never took my eyes off Slither as I got in the back. *Never turn your back on the devil. Never.*

Manic closed the doors, and only then did I relax against the paneling of the van. I closed my eyes, leaning my head back, focusing on trying to get my rage under control—trying to get the adrenaline to slow the fuck down.

"You should have let me kill him." Ink slammed his fist into the side panel. "You should have let me kill that son of a bitch!"

"Not today." Granite pinned him with a warning stare. "Not today, Ink."

"Why the fuck not? That was the perfect opportunity to fucking take them out, and you let them get away."

"You're too angry," I said without looking at him. "If you fight Slither with that amount of anger pumping through your veins, you'll lose."

"Like fuck I will."

Dutch swerved sharply to the right, and I had to steady myself as I looked over to Granite. The confidence that always clung to him like a second skin was gone, his face no longer as hardened as it used to be. With his fingers weaved through his hair, his gaze cut from Ink to the floor. I already knew what thoughts ran through his mind, what it was that had him looking so despondent and pale.

"He won't hurt anyone else."

Granite looked up at me, the green in his eyes now a sullen gray.

"Slither will never hurt anyone else we care about. I promise." I sat up straight and looked at each of the guys. "Not while I'm president."

WRAITH

The Hanged Man wasn't your typical American dive bar. From the outside, it didn't look like much. If you didn't know it was a bar, you wouldn't have been able to guess it. Not by looking at the black tinted windows and the steel door that seemed like it had been bolted shut. But I knew what went on behind that door, how wild MC parties could get. It was usually nothing short of barbaric, a bunch of savages drinking their weight in alcohol, getting high, and fucking whores until dawn. That was all it was about. Alcohol. Drugs. Whores. And plenty of it.

Word on the street was the Kings had been laying low on their wild parties, being picky on who they let in without a proper invitation. Apparently, it had to do with the big bad wolf, Granite, being a little overprotective when it came to his old lady. And everyone knew about the war on these streets, so my guess was the once savage president had turned into a an overprotective beast.

Goodbye, wild parties. Hello, snore-fest.

It was almost ten p.m., but traffic lights and car engines

filled the night with life. New York. The city that never sleeps.

As I reached out to the door, I took a deep breath. Odds were, they would either welcome me as a potential patch-whore, or toss my ass to the curb the second I put my boots in that bar. But I had to try. I knew he'd be here. In fact, I counted on it. He admitted to following me the other night; it was only fair if I did the same.

The door creaked open, and I walked in, only to have an entire bar full of people turn my way, staring at me like I was fucking lost. Clearly, the locals didn't take well to new people.

Shifting from one leg to the other, I glanced around, painfully aware of every stare pinned on me. I suppressed the need to fidget, pretending to be confident enough to think I belonged in here as much as everyone else did.

Heavy rock music boomed from the speakers, but it didn't smother the whispers. Everyone was thinking it. I could feel it in the way eyes leered my way.

Patchwhore.

With self-assurance and poise, I made my way to the bar right across from me. I kept my plump lips in a smirk, hiding the teeny-tiny bit of insecurity that tingled at the base of my neck.

The bartender was young and wore a cut with a prospect tag at the front. The dark circles under his eyes told me he was having a pretty hard time trying to prove himself worthy of being an American Street King. Everyone who knew their New York City crews would know that it was nearly impossible to get patched with the Kings. Many prospects have tried and failed.

"Jack Daniel's on the rocks and a shot of tequila."

"Yes, ma'am." He smiled, grabbing a glass.

I leaned over the counter and glanced from one side of the bar to the other. There weren't a lot of women present, but those who were clearly were old ladies who preferred to cling to their men's side. I didn't blame them. Crew men were notorious cheaters, pussy being their main motivator in every damn thing.

"What are you doing here?"

I smirked when I heard the familiar voice. "Opal, is it?" I turned to face him.

"Onyx."

"Oh, snap. Almost had it right."

The lack of a smirk gave the impression he wasn't amused.

"Aw. What's the matter? Didn't have your dose of happy medicine today?"

He leaned with an elbow on the counter. "Are you following me?"

"No. Maybe. What if I am?"

Sky-blue eyes searched mine, studying me. The pure color of his irises made it seem like you could look right through them, get a glimpse of what lay beneath. But something told me the light shade of his eyes was a stark contrast to the darkness that lurked within.

"I'd say you should be careful walking into places like this one," he dragged his attention up and down my body, "but something tells me a girl like you can take care of herself."

I placed a hand on my hip. "Of course I can. Why else would I march into a bar like this one without a knight in shining armor to protect me?"

"Come, now," he started. "We both know you're not looking for a knight in shining armor. You're looking for a devil in leather."

I bit my lip. "If I am, will I find him here?"

Our gazes locked, mine fire, and his ice. The music faded, and all I heard was my drumming heartbeat, the look in his eyes intoxicating me with every passing second. There was something different about him—threatening yet captivating, and I felt drawn to it in a way I couldn't explain. It was disarming but electrifying at the same time. It was easy to see he was the wild card, the one who hated rules the most.

He moved a little closer. "There are a lot of devils in leather around here, sweetheart, but none of them are the right one for you."

"I'm a big girl. I think I can decide who's right for me and who isn't."

"You're naive."

"Excuse me?"

"You heard me." He shifted even closer. "You pretend to know the rules, walking in here like you belong in this world, but that look in your eye, it tells me a different story."

"Yeah? And what's that?"

He smirked, biting his bottom lip. "You're searching for something. But let me tell you this. Whatever you're searching for," he stepped right up to me, his face inches from mine as our breaths collided, "you won't find it here."

For a split second, I was frozen on the spot, enthralled by the man before me. The other night when we first met, he didn't seem as troubled as he did now. Agitation swirled in the blue of his eyes, a dark unease settling over him. I'd be a liar if I said it didn't make me even more curious about him.

Onyx narrowed his eyes, no trace of the roguishness I had experienced with him before. It was odd that he no longer wanted to partake in the banter that seemed to come naturally to us every time we bumped into each other.

There were worry lines on his forehead which he didn't have before. And the cold expression on his face did a pretty good job at hiding any sign of the carefree personality I caught a glimpse of the other day. But rather than deter me from playing this game with him, it only made me want to play harder.

With a sly grin, I turned to the bartender and thanked him when he placed my drinks in front of me.

"So, am I right?"

I gave Onyx a sideway glance. "About?"

"About you searching for something here."

"Are we not all searching for *something* in this life?"

"You know what I mean."

"Wow." I widened my eyes. "Why so grim, buttercup?"

Onyx straightened. "Not grim. Just curious."

"About what?"

"You."

I balked, smiled, then tossed the shot of tequila back without being even slightly aware of its sting as it traveled down my throat. "Believe me, there's nothing worth being curious about."

"I don't believe that. I've never seen you around these parts of town before, yet this is the third time in one week we happen to run into each other?"

"I know. It's really random, don't you think?" I turned to face him again, and his eyes pulled into slits as he studied me. "Your lack of a sense of humor is really unbecoming." I turned and glanced around the bar. "Where's that guy with the pretty scar on his face? He seems like he could be fun to hang around."

Onyx shifted closer again, and I could smell the spicy scent of his expensive cologne which contradicted his street look with a pair of torn jeans and a dirty shirt. My gaze drifted to the shirt he wore beneath his cut. Onyx wasn't a small man, muscles and brute teasing through the white fabric. It had been a long time since I appreciated a man standing so close to me, his large frame hiding me from the rest of the dimly-lit bar. Whether it was his smell or his presence, I didn't know. But I felt drunk after only one shot of alcohol yet managed to keep my stone composure from cracking.

"See something you like...*buttercup*?" His voice dipped low, but it wasn't any less powerful. This wasn't the man I met in the bar last week, nor the man I encountered while they were on their Sunday run. This man was different. Intense. And a lot more intimidating.

I kept my eyes locked with his. "Other than the bottle of tequila behind you, no."

He smiled, but it was as cold as the blue of his eyes, and it sent a chill down my spine. "You seem like a smart woman, Wraith. Which is why you should turn around and walk out of this place."

"I don't scare easily."

"You should."

"Why?"

"Because once you've descended into hell, there's no getting out."

I moved forward, lifting my chin as I continued to look him in the eye. "What gives you the idea I'm not already in hell?"

I felt his warm breath skid across my cheek, eyes glancing from mine down to my lips and back up. The corner of his mouth twitched, yet he remained unmoved. Still. Frozen. Just like me.

The bar full of people disappeared. The New York City

buzz vanished, replaced by something heavy and laden with tension, with a need to touch. To take. To use.

"Where did you come from, Wraith?" He leaned down, his face inches from mine. "Who are you?"

I could smell the bourbon on his breath, and mixed with his spicy scent, it was something I could get high on.

This was wrong.

This was dangerous.

You should run.

But I came here to find him.

Well, you found him. Now run.

I took a step back. "You'll never know."

My feet managed to move back and away from him. Step by step, I retreated before tearing my gaze from him and rushing out of The Hanged Man.

8

ONYX

I WATCHED HER STORM OUT. For a second, I contemplated going after her, but deep down, I knew the better option was to let her go. It was a good thing, the way she rushed off and away from me. Away from this place. I didn't need another person to care about—not with this war raging. And there was something threatening in her eyes, something that lured me in. A hunt for secrets, a chase for the darkness I saw lurking behind pale blue eyes.

Her scent still lingered even though she was gone. She smelled like fruit and lush forests—tantalizing and sweet, with a hint of mysterious complexity. If it was any other place, any other time, I would have had my hands all over her body right about now. But this was not the place, and definitely not the time. Not for me, anyway.

"Yo, Onyx. You ready?"

I turned and found Manic waiting for me by the base of the stairs. "Yeah, I'm coming."

Wraith's glass of whiskey was standing untouched on the bar. I picked it up and downed it with one large gulp, relishing the sting as it traveled down to settle in my stomach. Woman had taste in alcohol, I'd give her that.

Moving through the crowd, I approached the stairs and took two at a time on my way up. Ink emerged from Neon's room at the same time a shoe came flying over his head. He ducked and looked back into the room just in time for a boot to hit him in the face.

"Jesus, woman. Calm the fuck down."

"I said get out!" Neon's voice cracked down the hall, followed by the slam of the door.

I snickered as Ink came walking toward me. "Where's a fucking horse tranquilizer when you need one?"

"Why do you keep on doing this to yourself?"

"Doing what?"

We sauntered into the kitchen and out the back door. "Neon doesn't want you, man."

"Yeah, she does. She just doesn't know it yet."

All I could do was shake my head. The guy was a fucking masochist and refused to take no for an answer when it came to that woman.

As we passed Granite and Alyx's room, Granite came out and shut the door. "Onyx, wait up." He shot Ink a look that said, 'fuck off, please.'

Now *that* message Ink got loud and clear. Getting hit in the face by a boot was too subtle, apparently.

Granite turned to face me. "You ready for this?"

"As ready as I'll ever be."

"Listen, I'll admit there was a time when I doubted your place as VP. But Dad believed in you, and now...so do I." He placed his hands on my shoulders, trying his best to give me the most reassuring look any brother could give. "You can do this. And I'm proud to see you step up like this to protect the crew."

"Thanks, man."

"I got your back."

The bedroom door opened, and Alyx peeked out. "Everything okay?"

"Yup," Granite assured her. "Be back in a few."

She nodded then looked at me, smiling. Alyx was no longer sickeningly thin and pale. Ever since the whole Tanit ordeal, Alyx had become stronger, and it was good to see her take care of herself. It was good to see her with Granite, seeing how happy she made him. Not a single one of us could blame Granite for wanting to protect her. She was worth protecting.

I shot her a knowing look and walked off, following Granite across the outer corridor.

"I don't suppose I get your mini outside apartment now, do I?"

"Not a chance."

Dutch was waiting outside the door for us, smoking a cigarette. "We have a problem."

Granite paused. "What is it?"

"There's a new drug going around on the street."

I scowled. "Snow?"

Dutch shrugged. "That's what everyone's calling it. But three people died the last two weeks, and twelve have been hospitalized—that we know of."

Granite swept his fingers through his hair, pacing up and down while cursing. "Snow belongs to the Sixes on these streets. But their shit's always been pure. If it's killing people, it's mixed."

"The Sixes aren't behind this," I continued with his thought. I looked at Granite. "But I think we know who is."

Dutch didn't reply. But the way he stared at Granite with fury burning in his eyes, lips pulled taut, chest rising and

falling like he had the devil's anger burning in his lungs—
we knew who it was.

"Jesus fucking Christ." I threw my hand in the air before
placing it on my head, crouching down.

Dutch crossed his arms. "We have to end this."

"And we will." Granite stopped pacing, his gaze cutting
to mine. "We will end this."

I bit my lip, a sour taste lingering in the back of my
mouth. This vortex of hell was only getting bigger and
bigger, and Slither was sucking in victim after victim. But I'd
be damned if I'd let him destroy us.

"Come on." Granite gestured toward the door, and
Dutch followed.

"By the way, what happened to Ink's face?"

"Two words. Neon. Boot."

Dutch snorted then followed us inside.

Manic and Ink were already seated, and I walked right
up to my spot when Granite cleared his throat, glancing
from me to his chair.

"No, man. Not yet." I shook my head lightly, and Granite
got the message.

The door swung closed behind Dutch, and when all of
us took our seats, a heavy silence fell over us. No one wanted
this. Everyone knew this wasn't the natural order to do
things. But it had to be done. I realized this yesterday when I
saw Slither beating Ink, when I got so close to losing
someone else I cared about. I couldn't let that happen.

The gavel was on the table, to Granite's right. It only got
used when really important decisions were made—
lifechanging decisions. Other crews used their gavels with
every meeting. But not us. To us, it was fucking sacred, the
holy grail when it came down to passing our laws. The last
time we used it was when we made the decision as a crew to

kidnap Alyx and frame the Pythons. That was months ago when Granite hit the gavel, sealing Alyx's fate...and ours.

When everyone was seated, Granite cleared his throat. "I don't think a long speech is necessary. We all know why we're here and what needs to be done."

No one responded. Not even a nod.

"None of us knows our fate. None of us knows what the future holds. But what we do know, the Pythons need to be stopped. And that's exactly what we're going to do, with Onyx as our new president."

I gulped. It was a hard pill to swallow, thinking that I was about to dethrone my brother from a chair he so rightfully deserved. But I understood why it needed to be done. The Kings had been under attack for fuck knew how long now, and all my brother had left was his honor, and Alyx. He would protect Alyx, and I would step up to protect his honor.

Ink scratched his beard. "Who'll be the new the VP, then?"

"Granite, obviously," I stated.

"No."

I looked at Granite, all sorts of confused. "What do you mean, no?"

"I'm stepping down, Onyx. That means I'm not going to sit in this chair again. Ever."

"That's bullshit!"

"Part of a VP's job is to step in and make decisions when the president isn't around. I can't do that. I need to distance myself from a leading role in this crew."

"Oh, my God." I pulled my palm down my face, almost smiling at how fucked up all of this was. "I can't believe this. You don't even want to be VP?"

"It's not about what I want. It's about making the best

decision for this crew, which is why I'll be nominating Dutch for VP."

Dutch blinked with a look of surprise on his face. "What?"

Granite nodded. "If you take the vice president seat, and everyone agrees, I'll be taking your role as the club's enforcer."

I straight-out laughed. "This is fucking ridiculous. I can't even—" I leaned my head back and looked up at the ceiling in disbelief of what the fuck was happening right now.

"Listen, guys," Granite started, placing his elbows on the table, clutching his hands, "I know it's a lot of changes, but the day I took my dad's place, I vowed to take care of this club as best I could. Today, I'm doing just that." He leaned back. "I made a deal with the devil to save my old lady. Did I do the right thing? Yeah. Would I do it again? Hell, yeah. But even though this is happening under these fucked up circumstances, I know this is the right thing." He thumped his fist against his chest. "I can feel it in here. This. Is. The right thing. And we will make sure those Python fuckers bleed for all they've done to us."

Silence settled around the room. Like a virus, it infected the air around us, and the amount of tension that was raging among us was almost crippling. No one said a word, everyone lost in their own thoughts. Clearly, none of us wanted it to be this way, but as I looked at my brother, I knew this was probably harder for him than it was for any of us.

He looked at me, and I gave a slight nod to the gavel at his right. It was time, even if we didn't want it to be.

Granite took a deep breath, squared his shoulders, and placed his hand on the gavel.

"Everyone's had time to think about this. In the matter of

Onyx becoming the new president of the American Street Kings, Dutch taking his place as vice president, and me becoming the club's new enforcer, I say..." he glanced at me, "yea."

His words beat against my heart like a drum, heavy with the sacrifice my brother was making all because he was hell-bent on protecting everyone he cared about it.

Granite looked over at Ink, and Ink nodded. "Yea."

"Yea." Manic followed without hesitating.

Dutch's head was hanging down, hands clasped together in a fist on the table. It would have taken a special kind of stupid for anyone to miss the fact that this was just as hard for Dutch as it was for us. Dutch had been at the top of Granite's fan club for fuck knew how long. He loved my brother, respected him, and this had to be one of the toughest things he had ever had to do.

He looked up and right at Granite, saying, "Yea," yet his eyes said the exact opposite.

When Granite turned my way, I couldn't get myself to say that one simple word. I couldn't get it out of my fucking mouth because my heart wouldn't let me.

"Onyx," Granite urged, and I rubbed the back of my neck. This was one of the hardest votes I ever had to cast. It was such a simple word that carried so much weight, tearing me up on the inside.

I dropped my arm. "Yea."

Granite nodded lightly, the expression on his face unreadable. I never knew how he did that, how he was able to hide everything he felt behind the stone look on his face. But it had to be hell to hold everything inside, to never let an emotion slip past that cold, hard exterior he wore around him so boldly.

He picked up the gavel, and I was sure it was one of the

heaviest things he ever had to hold. And the second that gavel hit the table, the sound resonated with a dire thud, changing our future.

No one made a sound. No one moved. The moment was too heavy—for all of us.

Granite cleared his throat as he stood from his seat, letting his cut slip off his shoulders. He placed it on the table in front of him, his hand hovering over the president tag. After tracing a single finger over the fabric, Granite yanked it off, tearing it at the stitches. "This tag was on dad's cut. I didn't want a new one, so I pulled it off his cut after he died." He held it out to me, his eyes gleaming with sorrow, yet there was a hint of pride as he stared down at me. "Now it's yours."

I stood and hesitated before I took the tag from him. "Even though I accept this, doesn't mean I like it."

"I know. We all know. But this is the right thing."

"You keep saying that."

"It's because I know it."

There was a bitter taste stuck in the back of my mouth as I stared at the tag. "I, um…" I swallowed. "I'll always look up to you, Granite. And even though I'll be wearing this tag, to me, you'll always be the leader."

Granite shook his head. "No. You are the leader now, and you need to accept that fact."

He moved to the side, making way for me to take the seat at the head of the table. The fucking chair was taunting me, like it knew how hard it was for me to make this move. This final move that would seal my acceptance as president and my fate as leader.

Everyone was still silent, the heaviness of this moment weighing on everyone's shoulders. But as I took my new seat at the table, staring at the men who sat before me, it was like the penny dropped. This was really fucking happening, and I was now responsible for everyone in this crew.

Our crew.

My crew. And I would go on a rampage through hell in order to give everyone here what they really wanted. Revenge.

I placed my hands on the table, looking everyone in the eye, one by one. "Let's go fuck up some Pythons."

9

ONYX

EVERYONE WAS SITTING around The Hanged Man, drinking, laughing, talking shit. Alyx joined us and sat next to Granite, his hand draped around her shoulder showing ownership.

Ink and Manic had been parked by the bar for the last two hours chugging down one beer after the other, and Dutch had been chatting up the new waitress. Since the whole ordeal with Tanit, Trick had left the crew, unable to deal with the death of her sister. And with Neon still recovering, we needed to replace three waitresses but had no problem filling the positions since there were a lot of young women desperate for work around New York City. But the three waitresses had now become fair game among a bunch of horny bikers, and Dutch clearly had his mind set on a particular blonde.

"You okay over there?"

I looked up at Granite as Alyx stood and left.

"Yeah, I'm fine." I shifted. "So, what do we know about this new drug going around killing minors?"

He shrugged. "Not much. All we know is it's not ecstasy —at least not clean ecstasy."

"We need to find out as much as we can about this drug."

Granite nodded. "I'm one hundred and twenty-five percent certain it's got the Python stamp of ownership on it."

"Yeah, me too. Ink needs to get on this ASAP."

"I agree."

A loud cheer erupted from the bar, and we turned to see Ink gulping down a giant mug of beer. The more he swallowed, the more beer spilled down the side of his face.

"Yeah, we'll wait until he has the hangover from hell in the morning before we give him the order."

Granite laughed. "See, you're already good at this whole president thing."

"No. I'm just good at fucking Ink around."

As quickly as the racket started, it ended. The sudden silence made Granite and me look up, and we saw everyone was looking toward the stairs.

When I turned in my seat, I noticed why everyone was stunned into silence. It was Neon, making her way down the stairs with her crutches, and Alyx not far behind her. One stair at a time, Neon hopped down, refusing to let Alyx help her. Everyone could see the struggle, how hard it was for her to move down each step. But we could also see the determination on her face to do it by herself. To conquer those motherfucking steps like a champ.

Ink ignored the three beers in front of him, wiping his face as he watched her move. The look on his face was priceless. Something between admiration and fear. I could only guess he was blown away by her strength, yet scared shitless that she might get hurt.

As her foot without a cast hit the ground, and she looked

up at us, her forehead creased with exertion, every single person in that bar stood—including Granite and me. It was one of the most powerful moments within the club, watching Neon rise to her feet, moving forward, determined to walk and live again. For the first time, I saw exactly what it was that Ink saw in her, why he refused to give up on her... because she was a fucking survivor.

Everyone started clapping, her cheeks blushing with a faint shade of pink. And while we stood there cheering for her, a tear slipped down her cheek. The feeling that swept through my chest was fierce, strong, and I wanted to burst with pride. This moment defined us. *Neon* fucking defined us. The Kings. This was us.

Strength.

A crew was only as strong as its weakest member, and Neon might not wear a cut, she might not be an old lady, but she was one of us. She was family. And she just proved that our fire was nowhere near burning out. The show of her inner strength had become our best motivator to take back what was rightfully ours and to protect our goddamn family. No. Matter. What.

Neon smiled, her face still painted with shades of bruised blues and yellows. "What does a girl have to do to get a drink around here?"

Laughter broke out, and Ink approached her, holding a bottle of beer. I half expected her to throw another shoe at his face, but the look that crossed between them was impossible to miss. The expression on her face was that of sheer appreciation, and his of complete infatuation.

God, it felt good to see her rise above what had been done to her, a bittersweet reminder that giving up, sitting back, and allowing life's setbacks to define and ruin you was not an option. She might have been knocked down. Trampled on. Wrecked. But she got up. And here she was, ready to face the world once more.

I continued to clap as I walked over to her. Her eyes were gleaming with unshed tears. "I'm so proud of you right now."

"Thanks." She blushed.

"It's good to see you haven't lost that fire in you, Neon." I reached out to pull her in for a hug but stopped before I touched her. Uncertainty made me hesitate, not sure if she would want to be touched. But she smiled and nodded.

"It's okay."

I wrapped my arms around her and pulled her in for a hug, careful not to hurt her back, which was still healing from third-degree burns. "It's good to see you on your feet again."

"Dude," Ink chimed in, "give the girl some space, would you? Jesus."

I chuckled and shot him the widest grin I could muster. "Jealous much?"

"Not jealous. Simply...concerned."

"Whatever, man." I placed a hand on his shoulder. "Go grab the woman a seat."

As Ink led her to the table, the door to the bar opened, and a figure caught my attention. Her eyes instantly found mine, and I let out a breath.

"Wraith," I whispered. She came back.

I made my way through the crowd, never taking my eyes off her. She stood motionless by the door, her gaze reaching for me across the sea of people between us. I wasn't sure whether it was the buzz of the atmosphere around us or the magic I saw swirling in her irises, but as I broke through the crowd, I rushed to her. And without thinking twice, I grabbed her face between my palms, forcing her back and crashing my lips against hers.

It was insane. I didn't even know her. I didn't know who she was other than she called herself Wraith. I didn't know where she was from. How old she was. Did she have family around here? I knew nothing about her. All I knew was I wanted to kiss her. So, I did.

I felt her hesitate, pulling back slightly. But I held her face between my hands, refusing to let go, and I forced my tongue through the barrier of her lips while fusing my mouth to hers, desperate to taste her. It felt like I was on a high I had never been on before, this kiss of a stranger forcing a kind of rush through my body I couldn't explain.

I continued to push her back, into a corner cast in shadows, hiding us from the rest of the bar.

She didn't touch me, but she kissed me back. Her tongue lapped against mine as if she was searching for my taste like I was hunting for hers. She tasted sweet, like oranges, with a subtle trace of mint and heat all swept together in one mind-blowing kiss. The thrill, the thirst, and the urge to never stop was overwhelming. It had my insides tangled up in a vise of desire and hunger, a need to explore and push the limit with this woman who simply walked into my life uninvited.

Her gentle moans might as well have been a wrecking ball, slamming against my chest, breaking my self-control into nothing but shattered pieces of lust. It was driving me mad, and I had to tear my lips from hers in order to catch my breath. Leaning my head against hers, I didn't open my eyes. "Who. Are you?"

"I'm not sure anymore." Her breathing was as labored as mine, hot and heady.

"I've never seen you before, yet now I see you everywhere I go. Why is that?" My hips flexed, wanting to feel the welcome pressure of her body against mine. Her only response was a soft whimper that rolled over her tempting, plump lips.

"Why did you come back?"

"I don't know. It just felt like I had to see you again."

"Why?"

"I'm reckless."

I moved my hand to her neck, my thumb gently stroking the hollow at the base of her throat. "Reckless is what I do, baby girl."

Leaning down, I kissed her again, covering her lips with mine. This time, I executed an insane amount of restraint, kissing her slowly and softly. But she met my gentle kiss with a nip of her teeth, biting my bottom lip, sending an electric jolt down my spine, crashing against my goddamn balls.

I reached up and yanked the back of her head as I gripped her hair in my fist. "You're playing dirty."

"And you're teasing me."

I licked my lip, tasting my own blood, my cock twitching and aching. "Not teasing. Taming...right before I break you."

She lifted her chin, those exquisite sapphire eyes shining with a dare. "I'd like to see you try."

"To tame you...or to break you?"

"Both."

I smiled while biting my bottom lip. "You've got trouble written all over you, buttercup."

"Yet here you are, desperate to get your fill of trouble." She leaned back and pushed her hips out harder against my cock straining against the zipper of my jeans.

"Gluttony has always been my sin of choice." I traced circles around her throat with my thumb.

She lifted her chin higher, exposing her neck more. "And here I thought it was lust?"

"Oh, I get the feeling lust will be a mutual sin for us."

Her confident expression wavered, like my words had become a hammer, shattering the air between us into pieces of forgotten desire. She peeled her gaze away from mine, and I hated it. I wanted those indigo irises on me, nowhere else. I wanted to stare into them and hunt for every secret she kept hidden, to peel away the layers and uncover the woman I had yet to get to know.

I took a step back, sensing she needed some space to breathe. "Let me buy you a drink."

Her eyelashes fluttered, and she pushed herself away from the wall, tucking a few strands of raven hair behind her ear.

"Come on." I gestured toward the bar. "Jack Daniel's on the rocks, right?"

A hint of a smile tugged at the corners of her mouth. "Yeah."

I held out my hand, and she hesitated for a second before she finally placed her hand in mine. With a warm smile, I tried to reassure her, tried to settle some of the thoughts that were currently wreaking havoc inside her head.

Guiding her through the crowd, my grip on her hand tightened with every step. As I got to the bar, Manic stepped up to us, a wide, smug-ass grin on his face. He leered at her from over my shoulder. "Oh, I remember you. Wraith, is it?"

"Yeah." She smiled. "And you're Manic, right?"

"You remember." His smile was as big as fucking Texas. "Can I—"

"Back the fuck up." I stepped in front of him, blocking

his view of her and glaring craters into his forehead. "She's off limits," I warned.

He raised his hands in surrender, but the smug grin remained on his face. "Sure thing, boss man." He winked at Wraith and showed some teeth with a smirk. Fucking asshole. I had to smile when he walked off. The guy sure knew how to fuck with me.

Wraith moved in next to me as we reached the counter. "Did he just call you boss man?"

Slightly uncomfortable with the topic, I pulled my hair out of my face, thinking of ways how to divert the conversation in another direction. "It's an inside joke."

Her eyes narrowed. "Okay." There was no way she was satisfied with my answer. "So," she started after I placed her drink in front of her, "why the warning?"

"What warning?"

"Last night, you said I looked like a smart woman, and that I should walk out of this place."

I raised a brow. "Yet here you are again."

She shrugged. "Seems I'm not so smart after all."

"Or you simply don't know how to follow orders."

"Depends on who's giving them."

The way her eyes gleamed, her tongue wetting her lips as she brought the glass to her mouth, it was all screaming sheer seduction. And I was falling for it hook, line, and fucking sinker.

"Tell me something about you."

"Like what?" She placed the glass down.

"Like what's your real name?"

She stilled. "Let's just keep it at Wraith, okay?" She turned my way. "Besides, it's not like Onyx is your real name either."

There was something in her eyes. It wasn't a warning, or

a threat. It was a plea, a desperation for me not to push the subject. It gave me the feeling she really didn't want me—or anyone, for that matter—to know her name. And that made me want to know it so much more.

Leaning on one arm, I studied her, my head already running in circles to think of a way I could crack through the hard bitch exterior...because I really fucking wanted to. "There's something about you that makes me want to figure you out."

"Don't waste your time." She smiled, yet it didn't reach her eyes. "Many have tried but failed."

"I won't." I slid closer, my lips already craving to kiss her again. "See, that's the thing about me. I love the hunt more than I love the game. By not sharing your secrets with me, you're only making me more determined to hunt for them."

She inched forward. "I dare you to try."

There it was. The magic fucking word. Dare. If a woman used that word around me, it was like flicking a switch inside my brain. That one simple word made my adrenaline spike, the thrill of the challenge prickling my skin.

"I'll make you deal." I kept her gaze. "A race. If I win, you tell me your real name."

She licked her lips, and I already knew she was hungry for the challenge. "And if I win?"

"I'll let you kiss me again."

A soft laugh rolled over her lips. "You're a confident man, aren't you?"

"I have reason to be."

"Oh, and you're full of yourself too."

I leaned in, my cheek barely touching hers as I pushed my lips against her ear. "I bet you want to be full of me too."

"Oh, my God." She pressed a finger against my chest and gently pushed me away as she straightened. "You have the worst pickup lines ever, you know that? Come on, let's get this race over with so I can crush that mountain-sized ego of yours."

My dick could not have been any harder than it was right fucking then. Watching her walk out in front of me, sashaying those curvy hips, made the challenge so much more goddamn attractive. Deep down, I knew I couldn't afford this kind of distraction right now, but what guy in his right fucking mind would pass this up? I'd be an idiot to— which was why I rushed after her.

The door slammed shut behind me as I stepped outside. It was a few minutes after midnight, the streets no longer crowded. There was a slight chill in the summer air tonight, and it felt good against my heated skin.

Wraith was already on her bike, fastening her lid under her chin. "Come on, playboy, we don't have all night."

"You really think you can beat me in my own back yard?" I grabbed my lid and hopped onto my ride.

"I know I can."

"Confidence is really attractive on a woman. I might just let you win."

"Don't you dare," she warned, starting the ignition. "If I win, it'll be fair and square."

"So, you *don't* want me to go easy on you?"

She pulled up next to me. "Nope." Her eyes met mine. "Give me all you got."

Challenge motherfucking accepted.

I looked down the road. "There are two sets of traffic lights. I've raced down this street enough times to know those lights are perfectly in sync with each other. One turns green, so does the other. At this time of night, they stay green for exactly thirty seconds. That gives us twenty-nine seconds to get from the first traffic light to the second before it changes."

She revved her engine. "First one to race across the green light wins."

"No. That would be too easy." I shot her a coy grin. "At the second green light, turn left. The back street will curve and lead us straight back here, coming from the other direction."

She scrunched up her nose, excitement beaming in her eyes. "Ready when you are."

"Let's do this."

We rode up to the first traffic light, and I revved my engine, shooting her a cocky grin.

Wraith remained cool, with a slightly challenging smirk on her pretty face. It drew my attention to the tiny dimple just above the corner of her mouth.

"On green." I turned to the front. Even though I'd love to kiss her again, I wanted to know her name. I wanted to know something about this woman who kept crossing my path—which was why I was determined as fuck to win this race.

The light turned green, and the roar of our engines cracked like thunder through the night. There were no words to describe the burn as adrenaline coursed through my veins, hearing the sound of her motorbike harmonizing with the sound of mine. The rush of air prickled my skin as we sped down the street, faster, and faster, and faster. I cranked the accelerator, keeping my eye on the green light of the second set of traffic lights. But by God, she kept close on my tail. I was so sure I'd win by a fucking mile, but she was fast proving me wrong.

I glanced to the side, the street passing in one big blur. All I saw was her at my side, her raven hair blowing behind her as she steered her Harley, handling that amount of power like a goddamn pro.

We made it in time to the second set of lights, turning left. But Wraith managed to get ahead of me as we swerved. Our engines sliced through the midnight air, excitement crashing against every bone. The back street was dimly lit, no cars or people in sight. With the curve of the road, I managed to catch up, putting us head-to-head on the final stretch back to the club.

The more I thought about it, the more I convinced myself that I'd rather kiss her again than know her name. What was in a name, anyway? Definitely not a mind-blowing kiss with lips that tasted like fucking heaven.

I snuck another glance in her direction. The thrill of the race was clearly painted across her face. The way she leaned forward, it was like she willed her bike to go faster, to fucking win.

Kiss. Name.

Name. Kiss.

I couldn't decide. I knew I could have gone faster and won this race. But I could not decide what intrigued me more. Knowing one of her secrets, or the idea of tasting her again.

We were getting close to the bar, the sight of parked hogs coming into view. I had to make up my fucking mind, decide what I wanted from her here and now. The memory of our kiss, her scent, the way her tongue eagerly danced with mine was on repeat in my head. But like I told her before, I lived for the hunt. I wanted to figure her out, and a name was the first step in doing just that.

Name.

Newly lit determination had me speeding up, going full throttle, the prospects of knowing who she was urging me to get my ass to the finish line before her. But she held firm, refusing to lose. If I ever had any doubt about my attraction to this woman, all doubts had now been left behind at the first goddamn traffic light.

Unfortunately for her, her determination to kick my ass at racing was slightly less than my resolve to piece the puzzle that was her together.

We burned rubber those last few seconds, but I came in first. Just.

She parked her Harley next to mine and took off her lid, her cheeks flushed from the rush. "For a second, I thought you were gonna let me win."

I shrugged. "I thought about it. The prospect of letting you kiss me again was real damn tempting."

She got off her bike, holding up a hand. "First, *you* kissed me. Second, you insult me by admitting it crossed your mind to let me win."

"I find it hard to believe a woman like you could be insulted so easily."

"Again with the *a woman like me*. Believe me when I say you don't know me...at all."

I got off my bike and straightened next to her. "Time to hold up to your end of the deal. What's your name?"

"Wraith."

I took a step toward her. "Your real name. And don't lie to me. I'm a very good judge of character."

"Oh, I highly doubt that."

Another step forward, and I put myself within breathing distance from her. She had to crane her neck to look up at me, her small frame lost in my shadow caused by the street-light behind me. "Your name." It was a simple request, yet an unyielding demand.

She sucked her plump bottom lip into her mouth, the

color in her eyes intensifying. For a second, I regretted my decision to not let her win because I really wanted to kiss her again, to be the one biting that fucking tempting bottom lip.

"Dahlia." Her voice was soft, her stone demeanor faltering for a second. "Dahlia Knight."

I smiled. "Dahlia. It's pretty." I reached out, gently tucking a strand of hair behind her ear. "Dahlia," I whispered, wanting to feel her name brush against my lips one more time.

The way she stared up at me, her eyes painted the opposite picture of the tough-as-nails image she tried to portray. It was someone completely different staring back at.

Her throat bobbed subtly as she swallowed, her lips glistening with sweet temptation. I was a strong man; I never doubted that. But right here, right now, I was weak with the urge to kiss her again.

I dropped my hand to her waist and pulled her closer, crashing my lips against hers. The taste of her exploded in my mouth, uncontrollable desire blasting right through my entire body. My chest, my stomach, my motherfucking groin —it all ached with a need to consume this woman, to take everything she had, even if she didn't want me to.

With my hands on her waist, I turned, pushing her against my hog. The moan that rolled from her lips to mine ricocheted down my spine, only adding fuel to the fire burning in my core.

I tore my mouth from hers, my tongue lapping down the side of her neck. My taste buds were drunk, intoxicated from her flavor. "Now that I know your name, I want to know more." Her hands were on my bike, her palms spread as she steadied herself while I pushed my body against hers as hard as goddamn possible. "I need more of your secrets, Dahlia."

The sound that came out of her mouth right at that second was as powerful as a motherfucking hurricane, sweeping through me with such force, it fucking wrecked every shred of control I had.

She lifted her arms, placing them around my neck, weaving her fingers tightly through my hair, kissing me harder.

Goddammit. It felt like there was this ticking timebomb between us about to go off at any second, and we had to consume each other as much as fucking possible before it exploded.

My hands moved up her waist, and I didn't think twice before reaching for her breast, palming it, kneading it, and not being fucking gentle about it. I was too lost. Too possessed with hunger and lust, wanting to bury myself inside her among all the secrets she kept hidden.

"Onyx," she whispered as I sucked the skin in her neck, my palm still working her perfectly sized tit. "We can't—"

"Don't stop me." I moved my lips up to her ear, my tongue sliding across her skin. "For the love of Christ, do not tell me to stop."

Her hips bucked, moved, like she was searching for something—something I was real desperate to give her. A groan echoed from the back of my throat, and when I felt her push her chest out, liking the way I touched and played with her tits, I lost it.

Grabbing her waist and twisting her around, pushing my chest flush against her back, I wrapped my arm around her, reaching up to her throat.

I dropped my other hand down her waist, and cupped her pussy through her jeans. With my lips against her ear and her sweet scent wrapped around me, I murmured, "If I had to slip my hand into your pants, what would I find?"

I felt her throat move as she swallowed. "What do you think?"

All it took was a flick of my wrist to pop the button of her jeans. She sucked in a breath, and I smiled with goddamn victory. "I bet your panties are soaked."

"Who says I'm wearing any panties?"

"Jesus, woman." I closed my eyes and groaned before slipping my hand down her pants.

The second I felt her warmth, how fucking wet and swollen she was, I thrust my hips, pushing my dick against her ass, trying to alleviate some of the ache. God, it felt like my cock was about to burst—pun fucking intended.

She reached up, wrapping her arm around my shoulder, and spread her legs slightly, as much as she could while standing. Her body had taken over, and it wanted me inside her. It wanted me to give her exactly what she needed.

Reaching deeper, I pushed a finger inside her, and her body tensed against mine.

"I'm not who you think I am," she said between labored breaths. "I'm not—"

With a yank, I jerked my hand out of her pants, placing a wet finger soaked in her arousal against her lips. "Shut up. I love your mouth, but right now I need you to shut it."

She bit her bottom lip, and my hand was right back in her pants, stroking back and forth through her folds while teasing against her entrance with the tip of my finger.

She exhaled sharply when I filled her with two fingers, her hips moving on their own accord. "That's right, buttercup. Fuck my fingers like you own it."

"Onyx," she moaned, her head lolling back against my shoulder. My cock was hard and ready, and I wanted to fuck this woman right here over my goddamn Harley. But I wanted her cum on my fingers first. I wanted to feel her pleasure gush into my palm while her cathartic moans dripped from her lips.

My thumb found her clit, and I circled the nub gently, giving just enough to take her to the brink of madness, yet not enough to push her over the edge. I wanted to play with her some more, torment her body until she could no longer fucking breathe.

"Please," she started to beg, her sweet plea feathering like a melody against my ear.

"I love how you beg." I continued to thrust my cock against her ass, the friction no longer alleviating, but intensifying the ache. God, dry humping was never my style, but right now it was everything and more, having her body against mine. Having my hand palming the apex of her thighs.

"Let me feel you come on my fingers." I pushed my thumb harder against her core, working her entrance. Moans rolled off her tongue and across her lips, her legs shaking as her climax started to build until I felt her inner walls tensed and her entire body went rigid as her orgasm peaked.

"That's my girl." I continued to finger and touch her, determined to milk every last drop of pleasure from her body. Feeling her tremble with the last tremors of her orgasm was like an aphrodisiac straight from the belly of Aphrodite. Powerful. Potent. Intense. I didn't think I'd ever wanted a woman as much as I wanted her.

I forced her face up to mine by wrapping my fingers around her throat, and I kissed her gently, teasing my tongue against her lips. Her labored breaths collided and mixed with mine, and I wanted to swallow every rush of air from her mouth.

"You shouldn't have come back," I murmured against her lips. "You should have walked away while you had the chance."

"Why?" Her voice was low and soft. Breathy.

"Because you won't get that chance again." My tongue lapped against hers, exploring her taste while my hand remained between her legs—wet and slick.

"I want to take you to my room, Dahlia. I want to take my sweet time worshiping every inch of your body until you beg me to fuck you."

Her body went rigid and her breathing stopped, no longer moving across my lips. "I can't do this." She pulled back, but I kept her in place, kept her from pulling away from me.

"What's wrong?"

She shuddered, and her lower lip quivered.

"Jesus, Wraith. What's wrong? What did I do?"

"Let go of me!" She yanked to the side, and I loosened my grip around her. "This was a mistake." Her voice trembled as she fastened the button of her jeans. Her hands were shaking uncontrollably, and she kept moving back, farther and farther away from me.

"Wraith, stop. What's going on?"

"Nothing. Nothing." She placed a palm on her forehead, her eyes gleaming with unshed tears. There was no trace of the blush she had on her cheeks earlier, her face pale and expression pained. "I have to go. This was...oh, God, this was a mistake."

"Wraith, calm down." I moved closer, and she kept shaking her head like I was a goddamn disease about to infect her if I got any closer. "Wraith."

"I have to go." A tear slipped down her cheek, and that one drop of sadness cracked through my chest.

"What the fuck is happening right now?" I was confused, my mind spinning at a million miles an hour. "What is going on?"

"Nothing. Just...I have to go." She got on her bike and started the ignition. My attempt at stopping her failed when she pulled into the street, speeding off without even putting on her lid.

"Jesus Christ!" I hauled ass and jumped on my bike, pulling out my phone. She managed to get away from me before, but not this time. Not again.

10

WRAITH

THE AIR SLICED like icy blades across my skin. It was summer, but my body was cold, my hair flapping in the wind as I sped down the road, not caring that I wasn't wearing my helmet. In fact, getting my head cracked open on the sidewalk would probably be less painful than what I was feeling now.

I let him kiss me.

I let him touch me.

I let him get under my skin and take control of my body.

The worst part? I liked it.

I liked feeling his lips against mine. His hands against my skin. I liked how his warm breath feathered across my flesh, and how it set free a thousand butterflies inside my stomach.

I wasn't supposed to like it so much. I'd never liked or wanted a man's touch like I did his. It was all wrong. It shouldn't have happened this way.

Scattered thoughts wrapped around my throat, making it hard to breathe. Every feeling that swirled around inside me was conflicting, creating havoc which slammed against my ribs. Onyx wasn't supposed to be the one to make me feel what I was feeling while he was touching me. He wasn't meant to be the man who would thaw the ice in my veins, yet he did it without even trying—without knowing he had to.

God, nothing made sense.

I swerved to the right, burning rubber as I sped through the streets. A glimpse in my side mirror was all it took for my heart to leap out of my chest. The light behind me was from a motorcycle. It was him. I just knew it.

Part of me wanted to slow down, to let him catch up with me. But I knew the best thing for me right now was to get away from him. He was dangerous. A complication that had the potential to ruin what was left of me.

I turned the accelerator, going faster, but he kept on my tail, refusing to slow down.

Judging by the pain in my chest, I knew there had to be tears, yet I didn't feel it, the wind sweeping them up or drying them out. Good. If I had to taste my sorrow, I didn't think I'd be able to be strong enough to try to get away from him.

The sound of his Harley got louder, and from the corner of my eye, I saw him ride up next to me. "Pull over!"

"Leave me alone!"

"No. Pull the fuck over."

"Go away, Onyx."

"Fuck!" He sped up and pulled in front of me, making it impossible for me to accelerate. He was blocking me off and slowing down little by little. Trying to go to the left, he moved in the same direction. He did the same when I tried to go right, desperate to overtake him.

What the fuck was he doing?

"Pull over!" He waved his right arm, but I didn't want to.

I didn't want to pull over only to look in those blue orbs of temptation—a temptation I had no business succumbing to.

I kept my bike steady behind him when I heard the sirens of a cop car. *Fuck!*

"Goddammit!" There was no other option. I had to pull over. The last thing I needed was more heat from the cops.

Onyx slowed down, and so did I, pulling into the parking lot of a building that seemed abandoned this time of night.

I hung my head down without switching off the ignition, my hands still gripping the bars.

"What the fuck, Wraith?" Onyx stomped in my direction when I heard the slam of the car door behind me. "Are you trying to get yourself killed?"

I almost fucking laughed. "You were the one who kept on cutting in front of me."

"Ma'am, turn off the motorcycle," the cop ordered as he approached us.

With a sigh, I switched off the ignition. I didn't look at him when he stopped next to us.

"Do you have any idea how fast you were going? And not to mention riding without a helmet."

Jesus. I did not need this right now.

"Onyx, next time you call in a favor, make sure you don't break a thousand and one laws."

I snapped my head in their direction, and I looked from the cop to Onyx.

"Yeah. Sorry about that." He reached out, shaking the guy's hand. "Appreciate it, though."

The cop nodded. "Remember you owe me one."

"Excuse me! What the fuck is going on here?"

"Ma'am, have a good evening," he said, all fucking polite,

like there wasn't a giant question mark on my goddamn face.

I got off my bike. "That was you?" I glared at Onyx.

The smug grin on his face was enough to answer my question.

"Jesus," I muttered. "Of course it was you. Goddamn Kings run this city." I turned and leaned with my hands on my bike.

"I wasn't about to let you get away again."

"So, you used a cop on your payroll?"

He shrugged. "A man's gotta do what a man's gotta do."

"Unbelievable." I sighed.

"Wraith, what the fuck happened back there?"

"Nothing."

"Like fuck, it was nothing. It was like you flipped a fucking switch."

I hung my head, closing my eyes. "The other night, you told me that if I knew what was good for me, I had to walk away." I turned to face him. "Well, now I'm telling you the same thing. If you're smart, you'll walk away."

"Yeah, see," he took a step closer, "I have this tendency to run toward trouble instead of away from it."

"That just makes you stupid."

He took another step. "And that makes you trouble."

I swallowed, biting my bottom lip.

"Why did you run away from me after...after what happened back there?"

The memory of how good his touch made me feel woke more butterflies inside my gut—a sign that this was all wrong and not supposed to happen. "Onyx, you don't know me."

"Running away from me every time won't fix that."

"My life, it's complicated."

"All our lives are complicated."

"Not like mine."

He inched forward, his scent surrounding me, and I sucked in a breath. "I'm not one of those guys who believes in fate and shit. But somehow, when I look at you, I can't help but think that this," he gestured between us, "was meant to happen."

If only he knew how fucking wrong he was.

"Wraith." He stepped right up to me, and I bolted to the side, away from him. Being close to him was fucking with my head.

His eyes narrowed. "What the fuck is going on? Did I do something wrong?"

"No. Okay." I pushed my fingers through my hair, leaning my head back and staring up at the night sky. "You did nothing wrong."

"Then what? Talk to me."

"I barely know you, Onyx. How am I supposed to talk to you? Just open up and tell you the soppy, sad story of my life?" Confusion collided with anger—anger I felt toward myself, toward the turn my life had taken, and how it was no longer my own. "That would be naïve of me, wouldn't you say? To take the secrets I had collected my entire life and throw them at your feet, hoping you can save me from my sad existence."

"No. All I'm saying is to stop running from me."

"But you told me to, remember? The other night, you told me to walk the other way."

He darted forward, right up to me, eyes burning with determination. "And I told you that was your first and last chance of walking away. You don't get another chance."

"Why?" I challenged. "A man like you can have any

woman he wants. Or are you one of those guys desperate to find a broken doll to fix?"

"Is that what you are? Broken?"

"No. Not broken. Destroyed."

His irises darkened, like he had just seen all my secrets. As if he had seen the level of my destruction. "You've been hurt."

"And being with you will hurt me even further."

"Then why the fuck did you come back?"

"I don't know!"

Onyx grabbed my arm and yanked me closer, pulling my body flush against his as his mouth came down, slamming against mine. His kiss wasn't gentle. His lips weren't soft and sweet. It was hard, firm, and it obliterated every inhibition I had. Memories of my past, the thoughts that always kept me prisoner, kept me from being with another man were gone, replaced by an inferno of desire. I didn't think it was possible for me to ever want a man's touch again. But while his tongue claimed every corner of my mouth, his hands exploring inch of my body, all I thought about was how I wanted more. More of him. More of this moment. More of...us.

I wrapped my arms around his neck, deepening the kiss, trying to tell him I needed more.

His palms gripped my ass, forcing me harder against him, letting me feel how ready he was. Like before, our kiss was achingly powerful, a frenzy of lust and a need to leave the entire world behind while we indulged in each other.

This was not part of the plan. Kissing Onyx and enjoying it was not part of the fucking plan. Yet here I was, kissing him, and so fucking desperate for more.

I let my arm slip from his shoulder, my hand traveling down his abdomen, feeling the ripped muscle roped across his stomach. As I reached for his belt, Onyx moaned into my mouth, a guttural groan echoing in the back of his throat.

"Touch me, and I can promise you there's no way you'll stop me from taking you."

My hand hovered by his belt while I heeded his warning, fingers gently tracing over his skin. I could feel his body tremble, feel his need radiate from him like waves of energy.

For the first time in my life, I wanted a man to take me because I wanted him to, because I liked the way I felt when he touched me. For the first time, I wanted to be with someone without having the devil knocking at my skull with his evil claws. Right here, with Onyx, I didn't feel the shackles of my past tying me down, making it impossible to move on. I didn't feel disgust, or regret, or wish there was a way to erase my pathetic existence from this world. So there was no way I would stop now.

I slipped my hand into his pants, and he groaned, his cock twitching as I took him in my palm, wrapping my fingers around his length.

Onyx nipped at my ear, his breathing loud and labored. He squeezed my ass hard, like he was starved to feel me, the anticipation building and building, promising to take us where we wanted to go.

It was liberating to be able to feel that, to feel the heat and fire—the thrill and the wantonness, rather than the pain and fear that used to accompany another man's touch. This was what I had run from earlier, the fact that it felt so different than what I had been used to. The fact that I liked it and wanted more. A damaged vessel shouldn't want to be filled. A used canvas shouldn't want to be turned into a masterpiece when it had nothing but black painted on it.

But this time I wasn't going to run, not while my body burned for him.

I wrapped my fingers tighter around him. "If you want me, then take me."

Without warning, he spun me around, his pants slapping against his skin as my hand yanked out. I was unable to breathe with the fire that burned inside me, his hands wasting no time in unfastening my jeans while his arms laid on my hips.

"Put your hands on my Harley. Push out those hips of yours."

I obeyed. I obeyed like a little slut, a girl who wasn't ruined enough to walk away from a man, and an act that would surely obliterate me. The inferno of lechery that burned with the flames of hell deep inside my core should have been a warning that I was playing with the devil. But I didn't care. I didn't give a fuck because, for the first time, I was doing what I wanted to do, and not what the demons of my past or the master of my present wanted me to do.

I placed my palms on his bike, and Onyx slipped his fingers beneath the denim of my jeans, jerking them down with a force evident of how much he wanted to fuck me right now.

The summer breeze skidded across the naked skin of my ass, and I sucked in a breath when I heard the sound of his zipper. "Do I need a rubber?"

"No." I could hardly fucking breathe. "I'm on birth control." I had to be.

"I was hoping you'd say that because I really want to fuck you bare."

My skin erupted with goosebumps when I felt the head of his cock trace along the slit of my ass. "I've never wanted to claim a woman as much as I want to own you right now."

"Then do it." I pushed my ass out even farther, my body primed and ready to take him.

He nudged at my entrance with his cock, and I closed my eyes, the anticipation almost too much to handle. I was spinning out of control, my body and mind consumed with a haze of intoxicating need.

"I really want to take my time with you." His voice was hoarse and low, and I knew he no longer had control. "But not right now. Not when your body is so eager to be fucked."

I felt his cock slip down my ass one more time, and with a hard thrust, he plunged into me, a scream ripping from my throat as pain and pleasure collided deep in my core. His thick girth stretched me, filled me, completely possessed me, and I almost lost my balance, my knees weak and legs shaking.

For a second, he stilled, not moving while he remained buried inside me. He gathered my hair into his hand, winding it up around his fist, pulling at the roots while I tried to sink my nails into the leather of his Harley's seat.

Slowly, he eased out, and with a grunt he sank back into me, only harder this time, deeper, letting me feel every inch of him. He filled me to the brim, and I never knew it could feel this fucking good. Every nerve ending in my body felt electrified, every muscle taut and tense.

"More," I begged, and he tightened his fist in my hair, rearing back before plowing into me again. "More!" I demanded, ready to scream. "Stop fucking teasing me and fuck me."

He yanked my upper body up, and I shrieked from the pain in my scalp. "Don't tell me how to fuck you. While my cock is buried inside that pussy of yours, I'm in control."

He gave a few more thrusts, and I couldn't stop the cries of ecstasy that slipped from my mouth, thankful we were cloaked with darkness.

"You feel that?" His cock twitched inside me while his

hand slipped under my shirt, palming my breast. "That's me. That's my cock inside you. No one else's. And you know what?" He buried his face in my neck, his teeth grazing my skin. "No other man will come near your pussy again. It's mine now. You. Are mine."

A shriek tore from my throat as his teeth sank into my shoulder, the searing pain a sign he had torn through flesh. But the pain was like gasoline on a fire that was already burning me to nothing but ash.

Onyx's grunts filled my ear as he pounded into me from behind. My thighs were coated with arousal, his cock easily slipping in and out of me. The slapping sound of flesh against flesh echoed through the dark, a filthy melody our moans hummed in tune with.

His palm slid from my breast and cupped me between my legs, his fingers finding that sensitive bud that would finally push me over the edge.

I reached behind me, my back arched as I pushed my hips back even farther, trying to spread my thighs wider.

Harder, faster, Onyx fucked me like it would mean death if he didn't. And during it all, I realized I had never, ever felt so free, unchained, and unburdened.

Wet lips kissed up the side of my neck, his tongue lapping against my skin. I could feel my climax starting at the top of my spine, slowly rolling down, leaving a trail of pleasure to spread throughout my body.

I tightened my grip around his neck, and I flexed my hips back, meeting him thrust for thrust. With my eyes closed and my mind rid of any thought, I surrendered to the euphoria Onyx so expertly fucked into me.

It was beautiful. It was lovemaking.

It was raw. It was primal. It was downright dirty, being

fucked against a motorcycle in the dark by a man who was supposed to be nothing...but a target.

Placing my palm over his between my legs, I pushed harder, his finger working me from the front while he pistoned in and out of me from behind, pushing me to the pinnacle of pleasure.

My mouth formed an O when an orgasm rushed over me, a hurricane of euphoria tearing through my body.

"Fuck," Onyx cursed as I voiced my pleasure with cries. His body tensed behind me, his steady rhythm faltering as he lost control. His lips sucked on the skin of my neck, and I felt his cock jerk inside me, his release pumping deep.

"Jesus Christ," he breathed as he wrapped his arms around my waist, his dick still inside me. "So, here's the deal," he started, sounding out of breath while our bodies shuddered against each other. "I don't know what the fuck is happening between us. All I know is...you belong to me now."

11

WRAITH

A<small>FTER WHAT HAPPENED</small> between me and Onyx, I didn't want to go back.

Home.

Finally experiencing what it felt like to be with a man without pain, without torment, it was bliss. In those moments while Onyx transported me away from all my demons, I felt normal. I felt light. And going home would only bring back all the bad that would poison me again. I wanted to hold on to this feeling of freedom for a little while longer.

So I went back with him, back to the clubhouse of the American Street Kings. It was stupid and reckless of me, risking everything by going with him. But I couldn't stop myself.

As we walked into the half empty bar, I spotted Granite and the rest of the crew still drinking and laughing, the clock against the wall showing it was past three in the morning. The stench of spilled alcohol was sharp, empty beer bottles and glasses scattered around on the tables.

Manic came stumbling our way, clearly drunk off his ass. "There's the pretty lady."

"Ignore him." Onyx placed his hand on the small of my back, guiding me in the other direction. But Manic stepped in front of us.

"Are you two," he gestured between us, eyes narrowed like he was trying really hard to focus, "like, a thing now?"

"A thing?" Onyx scowled. "What are you, twelve?"

"No." Manic swallowed. "I am drunk, though. My friend Jack Daniel's and I had a little heart to heart tonight."

"Clearly. Just remember your friend Jack when you barf all over your bedroom floor in about an hour."

Manic blatantly ignored Onyx while staring at me unabashedly. "You're hot."

I snickered, placing my palm in front of my mouth while Onyx seemed like he was on the verge of choking the club's road captain.

"So, I'm going to ignore you and walk away before your friend Jack gets acquainted with my foot up your ass."

I couldn't stop smiling as Onyx brushed past Manic towards the bar. "Drink?"

"Dear God, yes."

He rounded the bar, reaching for the tequila on the top shelf and pouring two shots. We tossed it back without even blinking, neither of us cringing as the burn settled in our stomachs.

After pouring the second round, he placed the bottle back and leaned over the counter, looking me in the eye. "Tell me something."

"Like what?"

"Anything."

I shrugged, leisurely drawing circles around the edge of the shot glass. "I'm your typical stereotyped troubled girl.

Parents died when I was a teenager, and my brother took care of me ever since." I picked up the glass and shot the tequila down my throat. "I rode with some clubs, traveled around looking for peace, yet always finding trouble."

Onyx reached out and touched my arm covered in tats. "Do any of these mean something?"

"Some." I didn't want to elaborate.

"And the poison ivy on your side?"

I smiled. "It's a warning."

"What kind of warning?"

Our eyes met. "That I'm poisonous, especially to those closest to me."

Onyx's lips curved at the edges. "I think it's more like you can create an itch that's impossible to scratch."

I burst out laughing. "Oh, my God. Where do you get all these lame lines?"

"It's a talent."

"It's more like a curse."

Our laughs lingered in the eerie silence of a now deserted bar. It was the perfect moment. "And you. What's your emotional wound?"

He frowned. "My what?"

"You know...your *emotional wound*. Everyone has one. Like, you fuck girls with dark hair because they remind you of a mom who deserted you. Or you don't screw girls with blue eyes because your dead girlfriend had the most beautiful blue eyes." I waved my hand around. "You know, some tragedy that fucked you up and shaped you into who you are today."

"Is that what happened to you? Some tragic event make you go on the road alone?"

And just like that, he had turned the tables, shined the motherfucking spotlight on me.

I tried to keep a straight face. "I asked you first."

Icy eyes stared at me, studied me, like he was thinking what his next response would be. "What makes you think I have one?"

"Oh, I don't think you have one. You have several."

He shot me a charming grin, tucking a strand of dirty blond hair behind his ear. "Let's just say all my wounds start and end with this club."

"Yo, Onyx," Granite called. "Bring your lady friend and join us."

"Come on." The second his hand touched mine, I felt it. The butterflies. Something I hadn't felt in years. It caught me off guard, and I froze, unable to move, or speak, or even fucking think.

"You okay?"

I blinked, shaking my head lightly. "Yes. Yeah...I'm fine."

He gave me a reassuring smile before we made our way across the bar to the others, hand in hand.

Granite was leaning back in his seat, arm draped over his old lady's shoulders. "Wraith, right?"

"Yeah." I tucked a strand of hair behind my ear as I took a seat, Onyx slipping in next to me. "And you're Granite," I looked at his old lady, "and you must be Alyx, right?"

She smiled warmly. "That's right. How do you—"

"Oh, everyone knows who Granite's old lady is. You're like the first lady of New York City."

Her cheeks flushed, and she diverted her eyes. It was true. She really wasn't from this world, clearly still adjusting and learning that confidence was key when it came to survival.

Onyx shifted next to me. "That's Dutch, next to him is Ink." Both nodded. "And that's Neon."

The woman sitting next to Alyx gave a half-smile. "Nice to meet you, Wraith."

"So," Granite settled in his seat, "where you from?"

"I'm...uh—"

"Around," Onyx interrupted. "She's from around town." He looked my way, his eyes filled with reassurance as he squeezed my hand. He knew personal questions would make me feel uncomfortable.

I cleared my throat, squaring my shoulders, determined to act the part. Looking over at Neon, I smiled. "Are you someone's old lady?"

Ink coughed—loudly. Very loud. Uncomfortably loud.

Did I just pick up on some sort of vibe between these two?

Neon glared at him with a frown. "No," she replied slowly, like she was trying to get a message across. "I'm no one's old lady, and I don't plan to be." Funny, she was answering my question, yet she was looking directly at Ink, who seemed really fucking uncomfortable, chugging down his beer.

"Well, that's not awkward at all," I remarked under my breath, and Onyx snickered.

"So," Alyx's soft voice broke the uneasy tension, "what do you do for a living, Wraith?"

I grabbed Manic's beer and took a large gulp, ignoring the what-the-fuck look on his face. "I'm a..." I swallowed, "I'm currently between jobs." It wasn't a lie. But it wasn't the truth either. There was a thin black line between telling the whole truth and just a smidgen of the truth—I was currently tiptoeing on that fucking line.

"I've never seen you around here at The Hanged Man before."

My gaze caught hers, her eyebrows furrowed. Was she

trying to figure me out? Trying to dissect every word that came out of my mouth?

I sat back, tapping my finger on the table, not taking my eyes off her for a second. "I don't get out much."

Ink snickered. "Now, that's bullshit I refuse to believe."

Neon slapped him across the chest with a backhand, shooting him a warning glare. Immediately, he zipped his lip.

I noticed her hand was bandaged, and it was clear she was missing a digit. "What happened to your hand?"

All at once, the atmosphere slipped from casual to grim, like everyone was two seconds away from choking on the air around us.

Neon placed her bandaged hand in her other palm. "Some psychopath cut my finger off."

I snorted, glancing from her to Onyx, only to notice that she wasn't fucking joking. "Holy shit. Are you serious?"

"Yeah." Her gaze was downcast, her fingers absentmind-edly tracing up her inner arm. "I'm serious."

"Jesus Christ," I blurted. "That's insane."

When she looked up and right at me, I saw it. I saw the pain. I saw the agony. I saw the rawness of suffering and torment, a haunting of every bad emotion ever experienced by humankind. It resembled my own. It was like looking into a fucking mirror right that very second, and it was terri-fying. Disarming. Leaving me unable to take a goddamn breath.

"Jesus. Who the fuck would do something like that?"

Neon sighed then got up from her seat, Alyx following suit. That was when I saw her leg in a cast. Neon settled on her crutches, leaning forward. She didn't look at me. She didn't look at anyone. She just stared down to her feet. "The devil."

Two words. It was only two words, but I could feel the weight of it bearing down on all of us like a fucking curse. I didn't have to be a part of their crew to know Neon had been broken. Shattered into million pieces. I recognized it, because that was exactly what happened to me.

"Neon." I turned in my seat to face her, and she stilled. "The devil is only as powerful as you allow him to be."

There wasn't a hint of a smile on her face, but I was certain I saw a glimmer of light in her eyes. A sliver of hope.

Ink emptied his beer, slammed it on the table, and stood. But Neon stopped him by holding out her hand. "Don't, okay? I just need to take one goddamn breath without you hovering over me all the time."

Ink froze, and I immediately saw the regret in her eyes. The hurt.

"Just," she moved back, "give me some space."

Ink nodded, and it was hard not to feel sorry for the man. For a mean-ass motherfucker, he might as well have been completely naked right then—transparent in his feelings for this woman. Even with the heart of thorns I carried, I could see how much he cared for her. It was sad. For me, anyway, because I knew if Neon was half as broken as I thought she was, she'd never be able to give him what he so desperately wanted. Her heart.

Alyx followed Neon, and I turned back in my seat. "What happened to her?" I whispered to Onyx.

He let go of my hand and grabbed his beer. "We fucked up, that's what happened to her."

"What do you—"

"Where's all the whores at?" Manic chimed in with a slur. "There was a time this place was filled from wall to wall with pussy and floor to ceiling with tits. Fun times."

"Jesus, Manic." Onyx glared at him. "I swear to God, your ability to be an asshole just gets better and better."

"Yo, Ink," Granite called. "You okay over there?"

He wiped his nose with the back of his hand before downing his beer. "Yeah." He cleared his throat. "No. Fuck, I don't know."

"Give her time, man."

He simply nodded, eyes fixed on the empty bottle of beer in front of him, yet it was clear he was merely staring into nothingness. Granite gazed at him with pity, a certain empathy shining from his irises as he regarded his SAA. And I could practically feel the tension roll off Onyx and onto me. I had only been in their presence for twenty minutes, and already I felt the bond between all of them, a comradery that went so much deeper than a simple patch. They weren't just crew members, they were brothers. Just by sitting here, around this table and in their presence, I was starting to realize the American Street Kings wasn't at all how I imagined. The way Granite hovered over Alyx, the way he stared at her—it would have taken a special kind of idiot not to see how fucking dedicated he was to her. And Ink? I'd known the man for mere minutes, and I already knew Neon was engraved on his goddamn soul.

This wasn't something I was used to, this feeling of true loyalty—not because of fear, but because of respect.

Where I was from, respect wasn't earned. It was taken. Demanded.

Dutch got up, grabbed his beer, and slapped Manic on the head. "You should get your drunk ass to bed."

"Fuck off. You're not my mother."

"Dude, you don't even know what your mother looks like. For all you know, I might be." Dutch shot him a cocky grin, and Manic just narrowed his eyes.

"Fucker."

"Cocksucker."

A chuckle vibrated in the back of my throat, and Onyx laughed. The way he smiled, how it reached his eyes, it was mesmerizing. I couldn't look away, and I wondered how he did it. How he—actually, how all of them could look so happy when their world was cast in shadows and painted with blood. The only person who seemed detached from it all was Ink.

Dutch headed up the stairs, with Manic stumbling not far behind him. Granite got up from his seat and placed his hand on Ink's shoulder. "Get some rest, man."

"Yeah. Okay." He got up, and after he left, Onyx and I were left alone in a now empty bar.

He placed his hand on my leg. "Come on. I think we need to shower."

"We?"

The grin on his face widened, a wicked spark glinting in his eyes. My insides started to turn and turn, tighter and tighter, like a vise. There were a thousand warnings going off inside my head, telling me I shouldn't be here. But I didn't want to go home either. If I had to weigh my two options, I'd tip the scales toward staying here. With him.

Without taking his eyes off me, he reached out, gently tracing a finger down the side of my face. "Where did you come from, Dahlia Knight?"

The way he said those words, how his eyes seemed to see right through me, I couldn't stop myself from looking away. It was disarming, like the blue shades in his eyes were reaching deep into my soul, trying to snatch up all my secrets.

He took my chin in his hand and lifted my face to his before tenderly placing his lips against mine, kissing me so softly, like he was expecting me to break any minute. Every hair on my body stood up, waves of electricity igniting every part of me. His kiss was gentle and light, and it was nearly impossible to think a beast of a man like him could kiss a girl with so much affection. It almost felt like he...cared.

He pulled away, his tongue lapping against his lips. "I need you naked and in my shower within the next ten seconds. You good with that?"

There was delay in my response, a quick nod of my head right before he grabbed my hand and rushed up a flight of stairs, dragging me behind him. With every step I took, I felt the anticipation build, but it was stronger this time. Maybe because I now knew what kind of escape waited for me in his arms, what kind of pleasure he was capable of giving me.

I glanced around as we walked down a dimly lit hall. For so long, I'd imagined what it looked like inside the American Street Kings compound. But somehow, I imaged it darker, more ominous and gloomier. They were, after all, one of the most ruthless crews in NYC.

Following Onyx, I tried to take in as much as I could. Tonight, I met everyone who lived here—five men, two women. A few weeks ago, the streets were abuzz with the shooting of a woman who used to hang out with the Kings. Apparently, she kidnapped Granite's old lady, and he planted some lead in her chest, saving his woman. Her sister left the crew shortly after. New York was a big city, but when it came to motorcycle crews around this part of town, gossip and stories spread like wildfire.

We didn't walk too far down the hall when he stopped in front of a door, unlocking it.

As he turned the doorknob, I swallowed, my heart beating a staccato rhythm against my chest. The grating feeling inside my stomach warned me not to go in, not to let him lock me in that bedroom with him. But what else could possibly happen between us? I've already crossed so many lines, feelings things I had no right feeling. Onyx seduced me, played my body like a devil's chord...and I loved every second of it. Problem was, I didn't belong here. I knew that. But he didn't.

Onyx dropped his keys on a table next to the door. I hesitated for a few moments, only staring into the room while my stomach kept twisting and turning, tied in a hundred knots. The room was minimally decorated, the dark blue sheets on the bed unmade.

"No use hesitating now. You already know I bite." He gestured toward my shoulder, and I touched the tender spot. "Close the door behind you." It wasn't a request.

With as much confidence as I could muster, I walked in and slowly closed the door. The slam of the lock resonated through my chest, and my heart started to race, knowing I was trapped between these four walls with a man who knew my body like it was always meant to be his.

I took a breath, his earthy, woody scent lingering in the room.

The chair in the corner had shirts draped over it, a pair of boots placed on the floor.

I felt the warm summer breeze coming from the open window, and I could hear the faraway sound of cars and alarms as the early morning NYC traffic started.

Small, hesitant steps were all I could take as I walked farther into the room, closer to the wall. For some reason, I felt safer there, putting more distance between me and him.

Onyx crouched and pulled a knife from his boot, placing it on the table next to his keys. "You can put yours on the bedside table if you want."

"What are you talking about?"

He glanced over his shoulder, a knowing look in his eyes. "The knife you're hiding in your boot."

"Who says I have a knife?"

He turned to face me, leaning back against the table. "Somehow, I doubt you'd be hanging out at biker bars without a means to protect yourself."

I crossed my arms. "Who says it's a knife and not a gun?"

"Oh, I know you're not packing guns. If you did, it would be tucked in behind your back." He pressed his lips in a thin line. "And I had a pretty good look at your naked back two hours ago."

Heat spread from my cheeks down my neck. The memory of what we did earlier ignited a familiar ache between my thighs, my core already winding tight with anticipation.

"Take out the knife, Wraith."

We kept our gazes locked, the air between us laden with sexual tension threatening to break down every wall I'd ever built around myself. I'd be a fool if I didn't acknowledge the crackle of electricity between us, the undeniable pull I felt toward him. I'd never experienced it before, and it excited me, yet scared me too.

Without breaking eye contact, I bent down, unzipped my boot, and pulled out the blade. His eyes darkened, the temperature in the room rising as he watched me handle the knife then gently ease it on the bedside table. "You think you know me."

"Oh, I know I don't." He reached behind his neck, pulling his shirt over his head. "But I also know that I don't really care who or what you are, as long as you're naked and in my bed within the next twenty seconds."

Confidence oozed out of him as he stood there bundling up his shirt in his fists before tossing it in the corner. During our little fuck-fest earlier, there was no time for me to admire his body. But while I stood there now, staring at him, drinking him in, I had no choice but to let my gaze travel across his naked chest, taking my time to appreciate his body for what it was. Fucking perfect.

Both arms were sleeved with tattoos. Crosses, roses, skulls, intricate lines of inked words all spread from his wrist, up his arms, and across his biceps. The way the ink curved over his shoulders, I knew there had to be more art on his back. The images called me. It made my fingers itch to trace along the black ink, to see where it would lead me.

"Turn around," I said in a soft voice, wanting to see what secrets he had engraved on his back.

He cocked a brow, lips curved slightly at the edges.

He turned, revealing the American Street Kings skull covering almost his entire back. My gaze drifted down to the cross below it, the word STONE appearing below it.

"My father," he said as if he had heard my thoughts. "My father's club name was Stone."

He turned back to face me, his eyes iridescent, giving me a glimpse of vulnerability and grief. It wasn't something I was familiar with, feeling grief when it came to the loss of a parent. But simply by looking at Onyx, I knew it was something he had been struggling with for a long time.

"He died." I stated the obvious, and Onyx nodded.

I had to look away this time. The topic of dead parents wasn't something I felt comfortable with. In fact, it made my skin crawl and my stomach ache.

His leather cut was on the bed, and I noticed the loose tag next to it. "President." I looked up at him. "Why do you have the president tag?"

Briefly, his confidence faltered, his expression that of a man who carried the entire world on his shoulders.

I walked closer. "You're the VP, aren't you? Why is there a president tag on your bed?"

He rubbed his fists together, and I got the impression he wasn't comfortable about the topic. But I didn't care.

"You are the VP, right?"

He pulled his hand down his face, reaching to the back of his neck. "Yeah. Not anymore."

I narrowed my eyes. "What do you mean?"

"It's club business, okay?"

"Are you the new president, Onyx?" I had to keep pushing.

He grabbed the edges of the table behind him and leaned his head back as he looked up to the ceiling. "Yeah. Yeah, I am."

"How?"

"Listen, Wraith," he pushed away from the table, "I can't discuss club business with you. That's not how we do things around here."

"But Granite is the president. And it's not like he's dead or anything. Is he leaving the Kings?" What the fuck was going on?

Onyx brushed past me and picked up his cut and the tag, placing it on the chair. "I really don't want to sound like a dick, but it's none of your business, okay?"

My mind reeled, trying to figure out why Onyx would be voted as the new president. The VP could only act as president if the president wasn't around. The VP could only take the place of the president if the current president died or got voted out.

Oh, my God.

I slanted my head to the side. "Granite got voted out." It wasn't a question.

"Wraith—"

"Why? Why would the crew vote Granite out? What did he do?"

"Why are you pushing this?" Onyx narrowed his eyes. "If you know so much about crew business—and it seems you do—then you should know there's no way in hell I'll discuss any of it with you."

The expression on his face hardened, his sapphire eyes losing their luster. I had pushed him too far, and I had to back down before I screwed everything up.

"I'm sorry." I had to gain control of the conversation, and there was only one fail-proof way for a woman like me to do it. "I didn't mean to push. I'm just curious, is all."

Sashaying my hips, I moved toward him and untied the bandana around my head, letting my raven curls fall down my shoulders. Unlike other times, I didn't have to pretend to be attracted to the man in front of me because I really was attracted to Onyx—dangerously attracted.

"No more club business." I stared up at him from under my lashes, our bodies inches apart, yet it already felt like we were touching. "Let's just forget I asked." I grabbed my shirt and pulled it over my head, his gaze dropping to my C-cup sized tits. The hardened look on his face disappeared instantly, blue orbs gawking at me with hunger.

He reached out, grabbing my waist, digging his fingers into my hips. "There's something about you," he started, licking his lips like he was craving a taste. "I can't place it. But it's like you're already in my head." With a jerk, he pulled me against him, and I sucked in a breath, placing my palms flush against his warm, naked chest.

"I think I know exactly what you mean." I craned my neck to bring my lips closer to his. The way my heart pitter-pattered against my ribs, and how my skin already tingled with a need to be feathered with his kisses, I knew the walls around my heart were close to crumbling to the ground.

His eyes glanced from mine to my lips. "You're going to ruin me, aren't you?"

My heart stopped, the blood in my vein turning to ice. "What do you mean?"

A loud scream tore through the air, echoing from the hall. The fear that resonated from the shrieks slammed against bone, and it almost fucking crushed me.

"What the fuck?" Onyx yanked open the top drawer and pulled out a gun, rushing to the door.

My heart was no longer beating, but rather clawing its way out of my chest. A loud thud of scurrying footsteps came down the hall, and I grabbed my shirt, pulling it on as I ran out.

I looked from left to right when I noticed Alyx hurrying down the hall while tying her robe.

"Oh, my God, it's Neon," she yelled, and suddenly there were so many faces darting in one direction. I stood with my back against the wall, only able to witness the chaos while stunned into silence.

Onyx tried to open the door. "It's fucking locked."

"Move the fuck up," Ink ordered before rearing back and kicking at the door. "Neon!" he yelled before kicking again, and again.

I cringed when I heard the wood crack and splinter, Onyx and Ink rushing inside the bedroom. Neon's cries were clear now that the barrier had been broken down, her uncontrollable sobs. The absolute pain and fear that rippled from every cry splintered through me. What the hell was going on?

Ink dropped a string of f-bombs, curses dripping from his mouth like poison. Step by step, I kept against the wall, my shoulder sliding against the concrete as I moved closer, Neon's cries urging me to see what was wrong with her. The last time I had heard someone sound so broken, I was the one shedding those tears.

I peeked around the corner, trying to keep myself hidden. With my hands against the wall, I watched as Onyx rushed across the room, gun aimed, checking everywhere —the closet, under her bed, searching every inch of the room.

"There's no one here," Neon whimpered.

I moved up until I finally saw her sitting on the bed, Alyx clutching her tight. Tears kept streaming down her cheeks, a look of sheer horror on her face.

"It's okay." Alyx kept holding her, rocking back and forth. "It was just a nightmare."

A nightmare? What kind of nightmare would make someone scream out in such gut-wrenching cries? Her fear was real; I could hear it in the shrieks that ripped from her room.

"This is bullshit!" Ink slammed his hand against the wall, plaster cracking from the concrete. "How long, huh?" He turned to Onyx while Granite stood against the farthest wall in the room. "How long before we can kill that motherfucker?"

"Ink—" Onyx started, but Ink slammed another first into the wall.

"I'm so sick and tired of excuse after fucking excuse why we can't go over there and plant a bullet in every one of those fuckers' skulls."

"And you think that will make this better?" Alyx glared at him with rage burning in her eyes. "You think killing him will stop the nightmares?" She didn't take her hands off Neon's shoulders as she continued to console her. "It won't change anything. It won't take away her pain. And it will definitely not erase the memories."

Anger rolled off Ink in waves, and I felt it infecting me from across the room. I had never felt so much hate, so much fury emanate from one man. "It sure as fuck will make me feel better."

"This is not about you, you selfish ass!"

"Alyx!" Granite's voice cracked through the tension, warning burning in his eyes. "Take Neon to the kitchen. Make her some tea or something."

Defiance beamed from her eyes, and I half expected her to challenge him. But she didn't. His old lady had been trained well. You never challenged a man in front of his crew—everyone knew that.

Alyx got up and handed Neon her crutches. "Come on. I'll make us some chamomile tea." But Neon was still so shaken, her entire body trembling, she could hardly keep the crutches upright. Ink intervened, took the crutches from her, and swept her up in his arms, carrying her out of the bedroom.

I pulled back, my body flush against the wall outside of the room, and he didn't even notice me standing there as he carried her out. I looked at them as they passed, and I saw scars peeking out from her spaghetti strap top. I slapped my palm against my mouth as I stared at it, red tissue and raised skin. I had never seen such grotesque scars.

God, what happened to her?

Alyx followed Ink as he carried Neon down the hall, and I remained silently leaning against the wall just outside the room.

"He's growing impatient." It was Granite's voice. "If we don't do something, we're going to lose him."

"I know," Onyx replied. "But what do we do? We're low

on cash and resources since we no longer have the Sixes, and our little weed business on the side ain't cutting it."

"Yeah, I know. But we gotta do something, man."

"Like what?" Onyx snapped.

"You're the president now. You need to figure out what our next move is going to be."

I leaned closer to the door, turning my head to try to hear more clearly. If only I could get my heart to slow down and stop beating like a hammer inside my head, I might be able to hear a little more.

"Brother," Onyx started, "you know me. I would rush over there and cut all their motherfucking hearts out right this second without thinking twice. I want nothing more than to see those Pythons bleed."

My heart stopped. It fucking froze in my chest, the ice spreading across my ribs and down my spine. *Pythons. What do they have to do with this? With Neon?*

Footsteps hit the wooden floors, hard and heavy. "Maybe it's time we stop playing it safe," Granite said. "We've been playing it safe for weeks, and it has gotten us nowhere."

"I know," Onyx agreed. "But you and I both know we can't do that when our emotions are running wild. Especially with Ink. That man is consumed with rage. It's turning him into someone I don't even recognize anymore."

"You and me both, brother. But we can't lose him."

"What are you saying?" Onyx's voice softened a little, and I leaned even closer.

"I can't tell you what to do, Onyx. You're the president."

"Stop saying that!" A loud *thwack* clashed against the wall. "When you took over from Dad, things weren't as complicated as they are now. You had time to settle in, to find your place among all of this. But me? I got tossed into a motherfucking vortex of shit without even having a day to figure things out, to wrap my own goddamn head around all this. Now I'm asking you, not as the ex-president of the crew, but as a brother. What the fuck do I do?"

The desperation in his voice tugged at my heart, and I wished I could reach out and wrap my arms around him, give him some sort of reassurance. He was so conflicted, even a stranger like me could figure that out.

"Okay, listen," Granite's voice dipped low, "take a deep breath. One thing I've learned during the last few years is to always follow your gut. What's your gut telling you?"

There was silence, and I could practically see Onyx rubbing his palm across his beard while he was thinking.

"Maybe we should start with the snow problem. Figure out if our instincts are right, and that it's the Pythons who are behind it. That might be the opening we need."

Again, I stopped breathing for a second.

"Good. I agree. Dutch thinks he has a lead. That kid we saved a few months back—"

"Trent?"

"Yeah. Dutch thinks he might know something."

"Okay, good," Onyx responded. "We should discuss a plan of action in the morning at church."

"Agreed. Onyx?"

"Yeah?"

A few seconds of silence passed before Granite finally said, "You can do this. I know you can. You'll be a good president."

"Thanks, brother, but just know that if your woman and your goddamn word weren't so important to you, I never would have agreed to this."

"I know."

"I'll see you in the morning."

I was so taken by their conversation, the information

overload causing me to freeze. Footsteps came closer, and as I managed to gather control, trying to turn in the other direction, Onyx came walking out. "Wraith?"

Fuck.

I turned to face him.

He frowned. "How long have you been standing there?"

"Oh, I just got here." I let my arms hang down my sides. "When all of you rushed over here, I stood back. You know, not actually belonging here and all. But you were gone a while, so I came to look for you."

He paused for a second, blue eyes scrutinizing me before he looked down the hall in the direction where they took Neon. "She's really fucked up."

"What..." I swallowed. "What happened to her?"

He wiped his hand across his mouth, preoccupied by his own thoughts. "I can't—"

"Tell me, Onyx. Please." I had to know whether what I suspected was true. "What happened to her?"

His gaze cut to mine, and I could see remorse swirling in the shades of blues—remorse for what had happened to the woman they had just carried out of that room.

"She got kidnapped by a rival crew."

"The Pythons?"

An eyebrow slanted inward. "You know them?"

"Just like the Kings, everyone knows the Pythons. What did they do to her?"

He took a deep breath before letting it out with a sigh. "They tortured her." His eyes bored into mine with caution. "Raped her."

I sucked in a breath, my palm closing around my lips.

"They fucked her up so bad, Wraith. The things they did to her, it's too horrible to describe. Those sadistic fucks left her for dead, and we didn't think she'd make it."

"The Pythons," I muttered.

"Sadistic motherfuckers. But that woman is one of the strongest people I know, and she exceeded all our expectations. But sometimes," his voice cut off, "sometimes it just gets too much for her, you know?"

"Oh, my God." I stumbled back, my heart refusing to listen to what my ears were hearing. "You're sure it was the Pythons?"

"Yeah, I'm fucking sure." He said it like it was obvious, like there was no chance in hell it could have been anyone else. "Our rivalry with the Pythons goes way back. Fuckers killed my dad. They are ruthless motherfuckers, Wraith. You see them riding your way, you head the other direction."

I held up a hand, my stomach turned inside out. "I can't —" I stepped back. "Fuck, I need to go."

"What?" He reached for me, but I pulled away. "Why? Wraith, no. Stay. I want you to stay."

With a heart that was busy smothering with heavy truth, I looked at him.

"Please stay with me."

It was there, in his eyes, how much he wanted—no, *needed* me to stay with him. After overhearing the conversation between him and Granite, the way Onyx sounded like a man who carried the lives of others on his shoulders, it was enough to crack through the brick walls I had to build around myself in order to survive the world I had no choice but to live in. The feeling I had in my belly whenever I was around him, the butterflies, I could feel something stronger than pain, stronger than years of torment starting to grow with every flap of their wings. It was scary, and I wasn't sure how I would get my mind to wrap around it. All I knew was he needed someone to be with him tonight. He needed someone to make him forget the responsibilities he had been saddled with—seemingly against his own will. And, by God, I wanted to be that someone. I wanted to be the woman in whose arms he sought some form of solace. The despondent look on his face, the heaviness he carried that shined through in his eyes, I wanted to make it better. Be the one who gave him the same escape he had managed to give me earlier. Even though I didn't know how to sort through my thoughts after what I had just heard, the horrors one of his own had gone through because of the...the Pythons. Jesus. I couldn't even—

"Wraith," he reached for my hand, "I can see it in your eyes. You want to run from me again, but something is making you stay."

"Onyx—"

"Just this once. Don't fucking run." He placed a hand on my chest. "Listen. Here." He touched the side of my face, his thumb gently tracing along the top of my eyebrow. "Not here."

God. How could I not? How could I not want to stay? "Okay."

12

ONYX

I couldn't describe it. This moment. This space in time. It was like the world stood still when I was with her. Like everything else disappeared, everything bad and broken just didn't exist. And while she leaned back, so beautifully naked, raven hair splayed over navy blue pillows, I finally realized what perfection was. It wasn't beauty. It wasn't diamonds or gold. It was surrender. *Her* surrender.

Stalking on my hands and knees, moving over her, staring down, something deep inside my gut told me I would never be the same after this.

Trust your gut.

Hovering over her, I dragged a finger along her side, her body trembling. With leisurely circles, I allowed my fingertip to caress her skin, making its way across her chest, around the curve of her breast. Her eyes closed, and she arched her back, relishing my touch, her nipple beading.

My hand dipped between her breasts, tracing along the most exquisite tattoo I had ever seen. A lotus flower bloomed across her flesh, its open petals decorated with intricate lines and patterns, the faintest shades of pink and green touching the edges. But it was the image below the flower that fascinated me. Shattered glass in the shape of a heart, hanging from the lotus flower by what seemed like rosary beads.

"What does this mean?" I kept tracing along the inked lines. "Why the glass heart?"

"All hearts are made from glass, don't you think? Otherwise, why would it break so easily?"

My hand traveled back up to the flower. "A symbol of purity."

She swallowed. "Detachment."

"What?"

"It's symbolic for detachment, as drops of water so easily slide off its petals."

My gaze locked with hers. "Why do you need to be detached from anything?"

She bit her bottom lip and turned her face away from mine.

Gently, I touched her chin, urging her to look at me again. "Why does it feel like I need to—" I swallowed, unsure of the words that burned at the tip of my tongue.

"Need to what?"

"I don't know. It feels like I need to protect you somehow. I can't explain it. It's like this gnawing need knocking at my chest." I met her gaze. "But from what? From what do I need to protect you, Dahlia?"

The sapphires in her eyes glinted as if unshed tears were threatening to break free. "I love it when you call me Dahlia."

Lowering myself on top of her, I nestled my hips between her thighs. A perfect fit. Like I belonged there, like her body had been shaped and molded for me, and me alone.

With a gentle touch, I brushed a strand of hair from her face before lowering my lips to hers. I kissed her tenderly, my tongue caressing hers in a slow dance of seduction.

The more we kissed, the harder I pressed my body against hers, loving the way her heat felt against my skin, like it had the power to thaw the ice in my veins. I'd never experienced this before, where I wanted a moment to never end—to go on forever. An infinite moment that would forever define us.

I reached for her hand, weaving my fingers with hers before bringing it up, pinning it above her head, my body slowly starting to move. I felt her tense beneath me, and she arched her back, pushing her breasts against my chest. My cock was ready, and judging by the soft sounds escaping her lips, I knew she was too. But I wanted to do so much more to her. I wanted to bathe her with kisses, taste and touch her, tease her until her body couldn't take any more—until she begged me to give her the release she craved more than anything else in this entire fucking world.

"Onyx," she started, but I let go of her hands and moved down, peppering her skin with kisses, lapping her flesh as I traveled down her body.

I lifted her leg, bending at the knee, her inner thigh touching my cheek as I kissed her there. Her hips moved, my lips only inches away from her pussy, already glistening with need, the scent of her arousal threatening my resolve to take my time with her. The way she responded to me, the soft noises of desire that came from her tempting lips, was enough to make me go savage, taunting the animal in me.

"I really want to take my time with you."

"Don't."

"But I want to." I placed a kiss at the apex of her thighs before tracing my tongue over her outer lips. She reached for my head, fingers gripping my hair, and I could feel her desperation for more, to have me closer. But I wasn't ready to let her tip over the edge yet.

Her back arched again, her moans growing louder. "What are you doing?"

"I want this to last for as long as possible."

"Don't. Just...just do it." Her thighs clenched.

"Do what?"

She lifter her hips, nails clawing at my shoulders as she tried to pull me up. "Fuck me."

I stilled. "No. Not tonight."

"Yes, tonight. Now."

I glanced up. Her face twisted like she was in pain, her legs wrapping around me, trying to pull me harder against her.

"Dahlia," I whispered and lifted myself away from her body.

Her gaze found mine before she turned her head away from me. "Do it, Onyx. You know you want to."

"No." I grabbed her cheeks, forcing her to look at me. "I don't want to just fuck you."

"Then what?" she challenged. "Don't tell me you want more than just one night of savage fuckery."

I narrowed my eyes as I stared at her. "Is that what you think this is to me? A quick fuck and a few-second orgasm?"

She tried to pull away from my grasp, but I tightened the hold I had, digging my fingers into her cheek. But then it dawned on me. "You've never been made love to." It wasn't a question.

The gleam in her eyes told me I was right. Fuck. I needed to change that. I needed to show her that not all men used and ran. We might be savages who rule these streets, but here in this room, in this bed, this was where our women ruled. The only place we showed weakness—weakness to the women who owned our hearts. And, by God, this woman was clawing her way through my heart so fucking fast, my goddamn head was spinning.

I reached down between her legs, slipping a finger through her slick heat. "I need you to lay still and take it how I choose to give it to you."

"What are you doing?"

"You heard me. Don't rush this, Dahlia."

She kept her eyes on me, but the confusion was there in the shades of color in her irises.

Easing my hand down between her legs, reaching for her entrance with the tip of my finger, I felt her hips buck as she wanted me to slip inside. But I denied her that by pulling away.

"Onyx, don't."

I let go of her face, still reaching behind me as I traced a fingertip against the delicate skin of her thighs. "Why do you want to rush this? We've got nothing but time."

Without warning, she shot upright, grabbed my shoulder, and had my back pinned on the mattress, her legs straddling me. "You think you have control here?"

"I know I do." I reached up and palmed both her breasts. "It would be so much easier if you let me do what needs to be done."

"And what, exactly, is that?" She thrust her hips, her slick pussy slipping across my dick, sending a wave of lust crashing against my spine. My hands fell on her waist, fingers digging into the skin of her hips.

"You need to be worshipped and not fucked."

"Believe me, nothing about me is worth worshipping." Another movement of her hips, and I clutched her waist tighter before flipping her body to the side, regaining control and pinning her back to the bed.

"From where I'm standing, every inch of you is worth worshipping. Why don't you see that?"

She struggled against the hold I had on her arms pinned next to her head, but I tightened my grip. "Onyx, stop this."

"No. Tell me."

"Tell you what?"

I stilled, staring into her eyes, her secrets slowly surfacing. It was right there. All I had to do was reach out and touch it—get her to trust me. I sat up, not letting go of her arms. "Your emotional wound. You asked what mine was earlier, yet you wouldn't tell me yours. What is it?"

"It's nothing." She struggled again, but this time I tightened my thighs next to her hips, keeping her in place.

"What is it, Dahlia? Who hurt you? Who made you believe that men only fuck? Use?"

"Stop."

"Tell me!"

"No!" she yelled. "You don't know me. You know nothing about me, so stop pretending and just do what we came here to do."

"And what's that? Fuck? Did we only come here to fuck like goddamn rabbits and move on like nothing happened?"

She stilled. "Isn't it?"

I shook my head. "No. Not this time. Someone hurt you. Someone gave you reason to believe all men only used. Well, I'm not that someone, and I sure as fuck won't be the one who uses you."

She tilted her head up, raising her chin, a blatant show of defiance. "So, you're telling me you've never used a woman purely for sex before?"

I loosened my grip on her arms just a little. "I have. But

the feeling has always been mutual. Those women used me as much as I used them. But you, it's different with you."

"How is this different?"

"I don't know, okay? I don't fucking know. It just is. And I am not going to be one of those men who hurt you."

"Oh, my God." She breathed out. "You were the one who asked me to stay. You practically begged me to. And now you no longer want this?"

"That's not what I'm saying." I leaned down, my stomach touching hers—heated skin and heated skin. "What I'm saying is you have a choice here. Either you let me do this my way, or you get up and walk out of here. But I'm not going to be one of those men, Dahlia. Whoever it was who hurt you, I'm not going to be him."

Sad blue eyes searched my face, and I could practically hear all her thoughts, her doubts—feel the way she hesitated, wondering if she could trust me. For those few moments, I remained silent so she could sort through those thoughts and decide for herself.

A slight nod sent relief crashing over every muscle in my body. Truth was, I didn't want her to leave. And even though I had just given her that choice, I wasn't sure I'd be able to let her walk out of here if she had chosen to do so.

Now that she had submitted, I didn't waste a second. My lips found her hard nipple, licking and sucking, lapping against the beaded bud like it was the last thing I'd ever do. Cupping the round flesh, I squeezed, wanting more of her in my mouth. While I still straddled her, I flexed my hips, moving my body up and down yet keeping her in place.

Her nipple popped out of my mouth, and I licked my way from between her breasts, up her throat, all the way to the corner of her mouth. "Has a man ever made you feel good before?"

"Yeah, you did an hour ago in the parking lot."

I snickered. "I mean, like this. Unrushed, putting your needs above his own."

I felt her tense beneath me, and I watched her face as her eyes stared up at the ceiling. "I've always just been a *thing* to men."

My heart hiccupped in my chest, and I instantly hated every fucking man who made her feel less than a perfect woman. Less than worthy of more than some quick fucking.

I flexed my hips on top of her. "I want to change that tonight."

"Why? Why do you care so much?"

"I don't know. But in my world, a man doesn't need a reason to care for a woman." Leaning down, I feathered more kisses along her collarbone, loving the way her body shivered beneath me. "Grab hold of the bed post above your head."

"What?"

I grabbed her arms and pinned them above her head, forcing her hands on the steel bars. "Keep them there. Don't move."

I let go, gently tracing fingertips down her arms. Her eyes closed, lips slightly parted. Lips had never been so goddamn enticing. I wanted to kiss them until they were bruised and swollen...marked.

Reaching back as I moved to the side, I slipped my hand beneath her knee, bringing her leg up, my mouth finding the sensitive skin on the inside of her thigh. "I want to do this every night. Use every second I have to make you feel good."

The closer I got to the apex of her thighs, the more I could smell her—the sweetness of her lust. The scent that would make any man go savage.

With a gentle, soft stroke, I licked the outer lips of her pussy, and it earned me the most beautiful sound from her lips. God, she tasted like heaven, and it turned my mind into a haze of euphoria. Not even cocaine was strong enough to give me the same kind of rush.

Pressing both my palms against the insides of her thighs, I forced her legs open, spreading them as wide as possible, her sweet cunt blooming just for me.

With another lap of my tongue, sweeping the tip from her entrance to her clit, I used my thumbs to spread her open for me. "I want to watch you come," I said against her wet flesh. "I want to see your pussy gush with pleasure."

She was already swollen and ready, ripe for the taking. And, by God, it was torture for me not to ravage her by tearing through her body with my aching cock.

"Onyx—"

"Keep your hands on that motherfucking bedpost. Do not move." Using my tongue and the tip of my thumb, I sucked and stroked, licked and touched, playing with the goddamn paradise between her legs. I could feel her struggle, her fight to stop herself from moving.

Fighting the urge to go faster, harder, I worked her pussy with a steady rhythm, determined to make it last for as long as possible.

"I want to play with you until it hurts."

"It's already hurting."

"Not enough."

Straightening, licking her taste off my lips, I stared down at her as I cupped her pussy, wetting my palm with her arousal before wrapping it around my cock, giving it a few hard strokes, needing just a little relief form the ache.

Her back arched, her expression dark, wild—almost primal. The room became toxic with need, both of us crazed with a carnality strong enough to break us. Even though I wanted to sink deep into her, I wasn't done playing with her yet.

Grabbing both her ankles, I pushed her knees forward, moving my hips so the tip of my cock nudged against her center, slowly driving forward, slipping inside. Just a little—that was all I gave her. Just the tip. Just a taste. She moaned, arched her back, and craned her neck, her body desperate for me to sink in farther. But I reared back, pulling out.

"Onyx. Jesus."

I smiled. "I'm afraid Jesus ain't here, buttercup."

Slipping a finger inside her, a desperate moan ripped from her throat. It wasn't enough; a single digit wasn't what she needed. I circled around her sensitive nub, her leg trembling, shaking, and I could only imagine the agony she was in. The anticipation of an impending release slowly tearing her apart inside.

Wanting another taste, I traced the tip of my tongue around her sensitive folds, purposely avoiding that one spot she needed my touch the most.

Filling her with two fingers, I guided my tongue through her wet slit. The way her inner walls tightened, the muscles in her thighs tensing, I knew she was about to come. And even though I wanted to torture her body so much more, I was pushing my own self-control to the limit.

I sat back on my knees. "I want to watch you come."

She cursed and moaned while my thumb continued to play with her clit, stroking it harder, faster, knowing she would need more and more until her climax tore through her.

"Oh, God," she moaned, and I kept my gaze glued between her legs, not wanting to miss a single second of me making it mine. Her hips lifted off the mattress, legs pulled taut, and when I felt her pussy throb around my fingers, I pulled them out of her while my thumb continued to play her on the one spot I knew she was aching for me to touch.

Her moans slammed against the walls, and I watched her body shudder as she climaxed, pleasure gushing out of her, coating every inch of her pussy and inner thighs.

It was fucking beautiful. And it was all for me.

While her orgasm still lingered between her legs, I stretched my body over hers, and her body welcomed my cock as I slid inside her.

Buried to the hilt, I stilled. "Look at me."

She opened her eyes.

"Place your arms around my shoulders, and don't take your eyes off me."

Her throat bobbed as she swallowed, placing shaky arms around my neck.

"Don't look away," I breathed.

Slowly, rhythmically, I rocked back and forth, in and out of her. Not once did I take my eyes off hers, wanting her to know I saw her, and only her.

"I'm not just owning your body right now, Dahlia." Another thrust. "I'm claiming it. I'm taking every part of you, and I'm making it mine."

She bit her bottom lip, barely taking a breath. "Onyx—"

I pulled out and slammed back into her, causing her to crane her neck back as she closed her eyes.

"Look at me."

With hooded eyes and heavy lust, she managed to meet my gaze.

"I won't let any other man touch you ever again. You belong to me now."

She weaved her fingers through my hair at the back of

my neck, and all she did was nod—her only sign of surrender.

My body overtook my need to make this moment last forever, and my own desire for release possessed me.

Placing both my palms against her cheeks, I no longer had the strength to control myself. With a rush of undiluted lust, I moved faster, harder, claiming her over and over and over again, until I no longer felt anything but the crashing wave of ecstasy as I came inside her. My release stormed through me, crushing every inch of my body with a strength that could tear me in half. But I didn't once close my eyes, because I wanted to look her in the eye as I marked her. As I fucked a part of me inside of her.

"You feel that?" My cock jerked inside her. "Get used to it, because you'll be feeling that every goddamn day for the rest of your fucking life."

I kissed her, sealing both out fates, making it one. It was no longer her and me. It was us. It was so goddamn surreal —this woman who seemed to have come out of nowhere, how she managed to tame me so easily, like she had been born with the key to my soul, an angel destined to find me. But somewhere along the way, she got hurt—her wings broken.

My broken angel.

Tearing my lips from hers, I watched as a single tear slipped down her cheek, the only drop of proof I needed. I was right. Someone hurt her, ruined her...and by the pain that reflected in her eyes, I was convinced it had destroyed her too. But no matter what kind of fucking monster I was out there in the world, right here, right now, in this room with her, I wouldn't be that monster. I'd be better than that, and I'd prove to her that even ruthless beasts had hearts.

I moved, licking the tears from her cheeks, pressing my lips against her warm skin.

"Tell me who hurt you, Dahlia, and I swear to God I will hunt them down and kill them myself."

Tears slipped down the side of her face, her eyes shut and lips trembling. She opened her eyes, and I could see every ounce of pain she carried inside her. "Someone already has."

13

WRAITH

THE LAST FEW hours felt surreal. And while I lay there beside him, hearing his rhythmic breathing while he slept, my heart was pounding with unease. Everything was wrong.

Onyx.

Me.

Us.

The Pythons.

After hearing what the Pythons did to Neon, a woman every member of the Kings seemed so fond of, nothing made sense anymore. And these feelings I had for Onyx were unlike anything I'd ever felt before. It felt good, yet unnerving at the same time. And the guilt? Oh, God, I'd never felt this amount of immense guilt in my entire life. It was one giant whirlpool of conflicting emotions swirling around inside me, and I didn't how to deal with that. All I knew was everything had changed. Something shifted, and my entire life, my existence no longer made any goddamn sense.

This was wrong. Me being here with him, feeling all these things was wrong.

I eased out of bed, careful not wake him. I had to leave so I could breathe again. Get some fresh air and at least try to sort through the jumbled mess in my head.

I slipped into my jeans and pulled my shirt over my head. When I grabbed my boots, I looked over at the bedside table for my knife. Then I glanced at Onyx still sound asleep. It would be so easy for me to stab my blade through his chest right now without anyone knowing. He wouldn't be able to fight back—if I was lucky, he would die without knowing it was me. In that moment, I was his biggest threat—the new president of the American Street Kings at his most vulnerable.

My heart felt heavy with the thought, the gravity of my guilt pulling it down to the soles of my feet.

Unshed tears stung the back of my eyes, and I knew I couldn't stay any longer.

I inhaled deeply, loving his scent and hoping it was something I'd always remember. When I turned to leave, I caught sight of his knife on the table next to his keys. Just one thing. I just wanted one thing of his, so I took it, tucking it in the side of my boot.

I stole one more glance at him on the bed, the navy sheet draped over his big frame. When I walked into that bar and saw him sitting alone that very first night, I never could have anticipated how much my life would change.

"Goodbye, Onyx," I whispered and sneaked out of his bedroom, gently closing the door behind me.

The lock clicked, and I leaned against the door, letting out a breath, and my heart aching.

"Early riser?"

I yelped, grabbed my chest, and spun around, staring right at Alyx and Neon. "Jesus. You scared the crap out of me."

Neon smirked. "That happens when you get caught sneaking out like a cat who just stole a tin of tuna."

"I'm not—" I rerouted my thoughts. "Hey, are you okay?"

Neon frowned in question, and I crossed my arms. "Last night, I couldn't help but overhear what happened. That had to be some fucking nightmare."

Her face turned a pale shade of pink, embarrassment spreading across her cheeks. "Yeah. Sorry about that."

"No. No. Don't apologize."

Neon smiled half-heartedly. "No one can create chaos in this clubhouse like I can."

"They care about you." The words just slipped out without me even thinking it. It was so obvious, even to a stranger like me, that everyone here cared about her—about each other.

"I'm sorry," I blurted out, and Neon stared at me with confusion.

"For what?"

"I'm sorry someone hurt you." The sympathy I felt for her was so strong, it clawed at my heart. It was like staring into a mirror, seeing my own reflection, witnessing my own anguish. Every tear she cried last night was a cruel reminder of how fucked-up this world really was. And I felt for her, without even truly knowing her.

She pinched her lips, prominent lines appearing between her eyebrows. "Yeah, well...shit happens."

I smiled, recognizing the way she hid her pain behind snarky remarks. But her eyes said something completely different, and I saw it.

I rubbed my fingers across my forehead, diverting my eyes for a second before looking back her. "Just remember... the devil only wins the day you give up fighting."

Her pale blue eyes softened, a sad smile appearing at the corners of her mouth. "Gotcha."

Alyx cleared her throat, a subtle way to clear the heaviness. "Onyx still sleeping?"

"Um...yeah. I have this thing I need to get to, and I didn't want to wake him."

"Oh. You sure you don't want some breakfast? Word around here is I make some mean pancakes."

I pursed my lips, lowering my eyebrows.

"I know," Neon remarked. "Her never-ending smile and 'life is all rainbows and unicorns' attitude gets on my nerves as well sometimes."

Alyx chuckled. "Oh, my God. You are a horrible friend."

"Wipe that fucking life-is-good smile off your face, then maybe I'll be a better friend. Why can't you just be miserable like the rest of us?"

There was a playful gleam in her eyes, but she gave me a knowing look—like she knew I was running.

"Come on, Swan Lake." Neon turned with difficulty, trying to steady her crutches. "Wraith has someplace to be, and you have goddamn pancakes to make—which are terrible, by the way."

Alyx smiled, and she reeked of happiness.

I took a step back, about to turn when Alyx asked, "I guess we'll be seeing you around?

Suspicion tingled the back of my neck, her tone of voice suddenly dropping with the slightest hint of dislike. "Um," I turned to face her again, "maybe."

"Okay. I know this is none of my business—"

"Alyx," Neon interrupted, but Alyx ignored her.

"Onyx really seems to like you. I've been here for months, and I've never seen him bring another woman to his room before. I'm guessing you're, I dunno," she shrugged, "special to him somehow."

"Okay," I muttered with caution.

"It's just, Onyx is like a brother to me. I don't want to see him get hurt."

"Jesus," Neon muttered under her breath.

My eyes narrowed. "And you think I'll hurt him."

"No. Not at all. I just care for him a lot. That's all."

I scrutinized her, not entirely sure whether this was a polite or a confrontational kind of conversation we were having here. Maybe it was simply another sign for me to get the fuck out of there. "So," I started walking backward, "I'm gonna go."

I turned, hauling ass in the other direction and down the stairs. The faster I walked, the more it felt like I needed to rush. I couldn't breathe. I couldn't focus on one single coherent thought, and it felt like there was no longer any gravity keeping me grounded.

Stepping outside the bar, I took a deep breath, but it felt like the air got lodged in my throat, unable to fill my lungs. My pulse was racing, my stomach twisted inside out. Glancing from the door of the bar to my motorcycle, I stood there, unsure of what I needed to do. But for as long as I could remember, I knew where my home was, or rather— who. No matter what happened between me and Onyx, how it made me feel to be with him, there was a driving force that flowed through me like the blood in my veins, urging me to go back to the place where I belonged.

I CLOSED the door to my bedroom, and the click of the lock might as well have been the sound of my heart hitting the floor. I had always felt like I had this immense weight on my shoulders, and over the years, that weight had become a part of my existence. But today it felt different, heavier, like it threatened to crush me at any second.

Letting out a breath, I leaned with my head against the closed door.

"Long day?"

"Jesus Christ!" I jolted, placing my hand on my forehead. I looked over to the window, the familiar frame of a man hidden in the shadow. My window was set on the west side of the building, the morning sun not reaching my room yet. "What are you doing in my room?"

"You didn't come home last night. I was worried."

"I'm fine." I took off my jacket, tossing it on my bed. "If you don't mind, I'm tired. I just want to get some sleep."

"Where were you?"

"I was out." I tied my hair behind my head, placing my hands on my hips. He was still standing in the shadows, unmoving. Even though I couldn't see him, I could feel his eyes on me. It was burning right through my flesh.

"You could have called."

"I didn't think I had to."

"It's called common courtesy."

I rubbed my forehead. "Please, stop. I'm tired. Can we do this after I've had some sleep?"

"I have another job for you."

I scoffed. "I'm already on a job, or did you forget?"

"This is different."

"How?"

"I have a client—"

"No." I held up my hand, my heart suddenly lodged in my throat. "We agreed. No more jobs like that."

"It's a very important client, Dahlia."

I pulled my hand through my hair. "I don't care. You promised me."

"I know. But I need you to do this one last job for me."

"No. Okay? No. Our agreement was—"

"I know exactly what our agreement was. But things changed." He stepped out of the dark corner, and I knew by the look in his eyes I would have no choice in the matter.

I swallowed hard. "You promised, Glenn. You promised me this job with the Kings would be my last."

With weary eyes, I watched as he walked closer, his shoulders broad and eyes determined. "Like I said, things changed. Now we all need to adapt."

I bit my lip, my skin cold, yet sweat beaded at the back of my neck.

"Talking about the Kings," he rubbed his hand across his chin, "I'm assuming you spent the night there, so I take it our plan is working."

I nodded hesitantly. "Yeah. You were right."

"About?"

"Onyx's weak spot. He seems to have a thing for broken women."

A smug grin spread on Glenn's face. "He sure does. Out of all of the Kings, he's the weak—"

"The one with the biggest heart," I interrupted. "He's not weak. In fact, I think he might be the strongest one of them all."

Glenn narrowed his eyes, the grin still curving at the edges of his mouth. "Oh, dear. You're not falling for the wild one, are you?"

"Of course not."

"Good. Don't be fooled by those fuckers. They're part of the bad people."

"Are they?"

He balked, and his eyes narrowed. "What?"

"Are they the bad people? Or are we?"

He held his arms wide open. "Where is all this coming from?"

I shrugged. "I'm just wondering." I didn't want to tell him what I heard, about what the Pythons did to one of the Kings' girls. What my brother did to her.

Glenn lit a cigarette, his whiskey eyes etched on me. "What's going on with you? Kings getting to your head?"

"No." I didn't hesitate to answer. "Things aren't adding up, is all."

He walked closer, reaching out and tapping a finger on my forehead. "Stop trying to figure out what's one plus one, and just do as you're told."

My heart jackhammered against my ribs, palms sweaty and my head spinning in a thousand directions at once. I had never been afraid of him, right up until I walked into this room right now.

He stepped back, smiling. "Find out anything I should know?"

There was a lot he probably needed to know, but it felt wrong sharing what I knew with him, like I was betraying Onyx—which was insane because my loyalty wasn't with Onyx. It was with the man standing in front of me now. My loyalty had always been with him—after all, he earned it after what he did for me. He was my brother.

Then why did it feel so fucking wrong all of a sudden?

He pulled his lips in a thin line, lifting a brow as he scowled at me. "Dahlia?"

I had no choice. I had to tell him what I knew. I owed him that. This was why I made contact with the American Street Kings in the first place, why I pursued Onyx. He was the easy target because he had the biggest heart. He proved it with the deceased anorexic girl, as well as the kidnapped ballerina—the girl warming his brother's bed. The girl who offered to make me goddamn pancakes.

I licked my lips, my mouth stone dry. "Nothing. Not yet."

God, it felt like I was slowly being infected, something eating away at my flesh, my soul...my heart. What was happening to me? This wasn't supposed to be this hard.

Get in, get some info, and get out. Then live your life like you always have. No complications.

I shifted from one foot to the other. I wanted him to leave before he had a chance to see right through me. See the turmoil I was in by doing my fucking job.

"Okay, well, keep your ear to the ground. I don't want any fucking surprises."

I swallowed on the lie, praying he wouldn't see my deception.

"Now, I have a few things I need to do before our meeting tonight." He looked me up and down. "Make sure you look your best."

My heart sank to my feet. "Glenn, please don't make me do this. I can't—"

He rushed forward, grabbing my cheek, fingers digging into my skin. Wild eyes penetrated mine, his expression hard and merciless—as it always was. I couldn't remember when I last saw kindness in his eyes. It had been too long, and I was starting to fear the darkness had already consumed him.

His gaze fell to my shoulder. "What the fuck is that?"

Air rushed past my lips.

"Is that a bite mark?" He looked back up at me, eyes blazing with anger. "Is that a motherfucking hickey?"

Jesus. I couldn't breathe. I couldn't move. All I felt was

the pain as he dug his fingers deeper into my cheeks, and the fear that settled in my gut like concrete. "Glenn—"

"Did you let him fuck you?" He pulled me closer, his body flush against mine. "We talked about this, Dahlia. Remember?" Fury rolled off him, slamming against my chest with intimidating surges. "Jerk him off, suck his dick, but do not fuck him. Now tell me you didn't break the motherfucking rules."

"No," I replied with a panicked breath. "I didn't. I didn't break the rules."

He tightened his grip for another second, his jaw ticking and nostrils flaring as he studied me.

"Good. Because no King is worthy of my little sister. And those pretty legs of yours only spread for the ones I choose." He licked his lips, darkness oozing out of him like an open sore. "Like the man you'll be making yourself pretty for tonight."

"Please don't—"

"You will do this, little sister." He jerked my face hard, my cheeks aching. "You owe me that much. Need I remind you why?"

My stomach turned at the subtle reminder of why I owed him everything—including my life. It was a debt I'd never be able to repay, no matter how many jobs—or men—I did for my brother. I was fucking breathing today because of him.

"No," I muttered. "No need to remind me...*brother*."

"Good." He let go of my face. "Be ready. And wear something...red. Apparently, the fucker has a thing for whores in red."

He straightened his cut, boots stomping on the wooden floors as he walked to the door. "Oh, I know old habits die hard." He glanced over his shoulder at me. "But don't use my real name in the future. I hate that fucking name."

I touched my cheek where it still burned from his touch while watching his split tongue dance across his lips as he stared at me.

"Yes...Slither."

"HEY," I walked into the kitchen, Granite and Alyx sitting around the table, "have you seen Wraith?"

Alyx took a sip of her coffee. "You mean the woman who slipped out of your room at the crack of dawn this morning?"

"She slipped out, huh?" I grabbed myself a cup.

"Yup. I even offered to make her some pancakes, but she seemed in a hurry."

Granite leaned back. "Has my little bro been played?"

"Nah. It's not like that."

"Uh huh." Granite frowned at me. "Do you have her number?"

"Well...no. I do have this, though." I pulled out her knife, the one she left in the place of mine. "Seemed like she left me a little memento."

"Oh, my God. Whatever happened to flowers and chocolates, or even leather wallets?" Alyx took a bite of her pancake.

I snickered. "That's so last year. Knives and objects of torture are the new way of showing affection."

Both Alyx and Granite started laughing, and I chuckled.

"Do you know where she lives?" Granite placed his empty cup back on the table.

I smothered a soft, "No," by placing my lips on a steaming cup of coffee. Clearly, my brother was trying to prove a point.

Granite got up and gave me a pat on the shoulder. "Don't worry, bro, we've all been there."

"Ahem." Alyx cleared her throat. "You have?"

Granite froze, and this time it was his turn to hide a very subtle, "Fuck," while taking a sip of his coffee.

I snickered. "Burn, motherfucker."

"Fuck you." He turned around. "Come on. Apparently, Ink's already sitting in his seat waiting for church to start."

"Shit." I put down my cup and stomped after Granite. "After last night, I don't think Ink's gonna be a joy to deal with this morning."

"Do you blame him?"

"Of course not. All of us want to make those fuckers pay for what they did to Neon."

I was about to fall into step next to him when Alyx called me, and I stopped to face her.

"What's up?"

"I know this is none of my business," she started as she got up from her seat, approaching me. "But be careful."

"With what?"

"Wraith."

Pressing my lips together, I straightened. "What do you mean?"

"I don't know." She shrugged. "Just, there's something about her I don't trust."

"Like what?"

"It's hard to explain. I feel like she's hiding something."

I snorted. "Are you serious? Alyx, all of us are hiding something or other. Not everyone is an open book."

"I know." She pulled her hand through her hair. "Just... be careful, okay? Out of all the men here, you have the biggest heart. I'd hate to see someone break it."

"Uh...okay." I rubbed the back of my neck, not sure whether I was exactly comfortable talking about my love life with Alyx. "Listen, I know we had, like, a connection or whatever you wanna call it. But I'm a big boy. I can take care of myself."

"Okay." She stepped back, holding her hands up in surrender. "I just want you to be careful."

"And I will be."

I turned and rushed out of the kitchen, wanting to catch up with Granite. That was the weirdest conversation I had ever had with Alyx. I appreciated her concern but didn't like the fact that she thought my love life was open for discussion.

I caught up to Granite just as he reached the door. He glanced at my cut. "You need to get that tag stitched."

"I know. It'll be stitched before sundown."

Granite nodded.

Dutch and Ink were already seated when we got there. Dutch appeared to be uncomfortable as hell in his new seat as VP, while Ink just seemed pissed. The room smelled like leather, smoke, and trouble.

"Where's Manic?" I took my seat at the head of the table, and in the back of my mind, I wondered if I'd ever get used to it.

"I'm here." Manic came prancing in, a huge grin on his scarred face.

I studied him. "What's her name?"

"Jennifer. No," he froze, "Jessica. No. Fuck."

"Jesus—"

"No. It's not Jesus either."

"You're supposed to have a motherfucker of a hangover, but instead you're sitting here gloating over pussy."

He shrugged. "If you got it, you got it."

"Okay," I called. "Let's start this shit show, shall we?"

Dutch rolled his eyes. "Let's."

I glanced at Ink, his expression not cracking even a little. "Something on your mind, Ink?"

"Nothing you don't already know."

Granite and I looked at each other across the table. I hated that he sat so far away now. His place was next to me —or should I say, my place was next to him.

He gave me a slight nod, and I breathed in deeply. "Okay. First, Dutch," I turned to him, "Granite says that boy we saved from his mom's piece of shit boyfriend might know something about the snow going around."

He nodded. "Yeah. I talked to him this morning. The dealers aren't talking about who supplies the shit, but he's heard the Pythons' name come up in a few convos regarding the new drug."

"That much, we suspected," I muttered. "If the Pythons are behind this new lethal snow, my guess is the Sixes don't know about it."

Granite nodded. "Cocaine is their business, and they won't like it when they hear their new arms dealer is moving in on their turf."

"Just like they did on ours," Dutch said as he lit a cigarette, animosity dripping from his every word.

I leaned back. "If we're right, and the Pythons are the new cocaine suppliers on these streets, we can use that to our advantage."

Manic lifted a brow. "How?"

"There's no way the Sixes will let the Pythons slide on in and make a buck dealing in their trade. If we can prove it's the Pythons, the Sixes will be bringing war to their doorstep. And the enemy of my enemy—"

"Is my friend," Granite continued. "We'll get our business with the Sixes back, and we'll have an ally against the Pythons."

I smiled, and I could see Granite was feeling all fucking giddy inside with the potential our new situation presented.

"I got word that there's a shipment coming in tonight," Dutch said, putting out his cigarette and fisting his hands together on the table. "If it's true, my guess is the Pythons will try to distract the Sixes while all this goes down. Make sure they don't get word of it."

"Makes sense," I said, wheels turning inside my head. "We need to find proof, then present it to the Sixes. It's the only way we'll convince Crow."

"Hold up," Ink interrupted. "Look how the last supposed meeting with the Sixes went down. Who's to say the Sixes aren't in on this with the Pythons?"

This time Granite intervened. "I don't know how Slither found out about our meeting with the Sixes the other day. My guess is he has a man on the inside, keeping tabs on them. But I know Crow. He's been the president of the Sixes for as long as I've been sitting in that chair." He indicated my way. "He might be a filthy son of a bitch who would steal candy from a baby, but he won't compromise his product. Snow is his trade, and it took them years to build their little narcotic empire. He won't jeopardize that by selling shit that's killing people left, right, and center."

"Granite's right," I agreed. "Crow's an immoral fucker, but he's no snake. And the only reason he's buying arms from the Pythons is because we stopped dealing with them, making good on Granite's promise to Slither. If we can prove Slither is busy fucking Crow in the ass, we get the upper hand here."

"Fuck, yes," Manic blurted. "About fucking time things got back to normal around here—normal being the Kings in charge of this fucking town."

"And Slither?" Ink asked, his face concrete. "Let's discuss the part where he dies."

"Listen, man," I turned to him, "I swear to God he'll pay for what he's done."

"Funny, that's all I hear everyone say around here."

I didn't like the look on his face, like he had somehow become detached, void of everything except hate. Revenge. Justice.

"If we can get the Sixes on our side, I can guarantee it will end with Slither taking his last breath. Just..." I breathed out, "just be patient a little while longer."

Ink slammed both his fists onto the table, ashtrays and beer bottles clattering. "I told you, I'm running out of patience. Even though Neon is up and walking again, last night proved she will not be able to move on unless she knows he's dead."

"And you, Ink?" I asked, pinning him with my gaze. "Will you be able to move on after he's dead? Will death be enough to settle that guilt you're feeling?"

"Guilt?" He glared at me. "What guilt?"

"The guilt of not being able to protect her. Even now, with her being safe here with us, you can't protect her from the memories, from the nightmares. And it's fucking killing you, isn't it?"

His jaw clenched, nostrils flaring while his eyes killed me slowly with a toxic stare.

I leaned closer, practically bathing myself in the hate

that radiated off him. "I swear to God that Slither will pay with his blood, but I can guarantee it won't take away your guilt." I got up from my seat, not taking my eyes off him. "Nothing will take away the guilt."

He didn't say anything. But his eyes spoke volumes. He hated me, hated that he knew I spoke the truth. It hurt hearing those words, and he tried to fight the pain of the truth by detesting me—even if only for a few seconds. So, I allowed it. I allowed him to hate me because it gave him a temporary reprieve from what was really eating away at his soul.

Motherfucking guilt.

"Manic," I called as I walked to the door. "You're with me tonight, tailing the Pythons.. Granite, you and Dutch find out where this shipment is coming in and get us some motherfucking pictures."

Ink shot up. "What about me?"

I chewed the inside of my mouth, closing my eyes, hating what I was about to do to him. But I had no choice. First and foremost, my responsibility lay with the safety of my crew—even if they didn't see it that way. "You stay here. Neon needs you here."

"That's bullshit!" he called after me as I exited the room. "This is fucking bullshit!"

The animosity echoed in his curses. And it stung like a motherfucking bitch, the fact that I had to do this to him. But I cared too much not to.

15

WRAITH

Past

THE NUMBER ten had been iced with pink frosting on the homemade cake. The entire house smelled like chocolate. Mom baked the cake the night before while humming the happy birthday song, smiling as she made her way around the kitchen. It was a side of her we didn't see very often.

Happy. Loving. Carefree.

It was the medicine Dad had been bringing home for her lately. That was what made her so happy, turned her into someone completely different. Before she started taking it, she was always sad or angry, either crying herself to sleep, or storming through the house yelling at everyone, cursing me and my brother for ever being born. The days she was angry, she said it was our fault. The days she was sad, it was Dad's fault.

But whenever she was happy, Dad was happy. And that made me happy. But not Glenn. Not my older brother. When Mom and Dad were happy, they'd have friends over, and Glenn didn't like it when other people came to our house. He never told me why, always saying he didn't trust other people. Said he only trusted me. His little sister. When we were home alone, that was when he smiled. He was the only thirteen-year-old boy in the neighborhood who liked playing with his little sister—always spending time with me whenever he got the chance.

Mom and Dad didn't have enough money to buy toys, but Glenn always found a way to make me something to play with. Like paper airplanes or using money he earned by washing the neighbors' cars to buy me balloons or crayons. But it was always our secret. He made me swear Mom and Dad would never know about the things he made or bought me. I never knew why, but I was too glad for the spoils to ask questions. I just nodded and played.

Mom placed a few paper plates on the table. "Happy birthday, sweetheart." She smiled. I loved it when she smiled. She looked so pretty, wearing a red dress that matched her lipstick. With her raven curls and pale complexion, I always thought she looked like Snow White. Only prettier.

"Blow out your candles and make a wish."

I glanced around the room. "Can't we wait until Dad gets home?"

"Dad won't be home for another hour, sweetheart. And I'm dying for a piece of that chocolate cake. Besides," she took my hand in hers, clutching it tightly, "he's bringing home another surprise for you."

My heart leaped with excitement. "A present?"

Her dark eyes beamed. "A present, yes."

"Did you hear that, Glenn? Dad is bringing me a present." I'd never gotten a present on my birthday before. It was truly the happiest day of my life. Birthday cake, a present, and Mom was happy. But Glenn wasn't happy, even though he smiled every time I looked his way. I could see his smile didn't reach his eyes. Why wasn't he happy? He was always happy on my birthday, even if Mom and Dad weren't. On my sixth birthday, he snuck into my room while Mom and Dad were still sleeping, holding a Twinkie with a single burning candle. He softly sang happy birthday so as not to wake Mom and Dad, and after I blew out the candle, I wanted to share the Twinkie with him. But he said he had a tummy ache. I still believed he lied. He didn't want me to share the tiny Twinkie. He wanted me to have it all, knowing it would be the only present or cake I'd get that day. Glenn always smiled on my birthday. But not today. Why? He knew how important this was for me, to finally have the kind of birthday I only saw on TV shows. After all, he had already had his happy birthday three years ago, the day Mom had last worn her pretty red dress. Why wouldn't he be happy about me finally feeling this kind of excitement?

Mom tucked my hair behind my ear, staring at me like she was proud. I had never seen her look at me this way, like I wasn't the worst thing to ever happen to her.

"Thank you, Mom."

She placed a kiss on my cheek, a show of affection my brother and I had hardly ever seen. "You deserve a present this year. You're my big girl now."

"What present is Dad bringing her?" Glenn's voice sounded angry, and his light brown eyes glared at Mom.

She stiffened, glowering back at him, and I didn't like it. I didn't want anything to ruin my happy day—especially not a fight between my mom and my brother.

"You'll see when Dad gets here." Her answer was cold. Clipped. The opposite of the warm touch of her hand against mine. "Come on, Dahlia. Let's blow out the candles and eat some cake. Remember," she smiled at me, "make a wish."

I nodded.

There were only two candles burning on the cake, but that didn't matter. Nothing else mattered but the happy feeling that filled my tummy with a thousand butterflies, flapping their wings like they were excited too.

I closed my eyes, and I made a wish. I even stopped breathing for a few seconds while I repeated the wish over and over inside my head.

I wish for more birthdays like this one.

Once I was sure my wish had reached the stars, I opened my eyes and blew out the candles. Mom clapped her hands and gave me a peck on the cheek. "My big girl."

I smiled, watching her cut the cake, placing it on the paper plates.

As she placed my slice in front of me, I looked up at her, and she nodded. It was one of the golden rules in the house, to ask permission before we ate our food—or in this case, the cake.

I didn't hesitate after she gave permission, grabbing the spoon and digging into the thick slice of chocolate cake, fluffy frosting covering the top and sides. I hadn't tasted anything like it before, the sugary sweetness of heaven that coated my tongue with every bite. It sure was no Twinkie, and the cake Glenn got on his tenth birthday wasn't as nice as this one—at least not how I remembered it.

Bite after bite, I ate that cake like it was the last thing I'd ever eat. Every mouthful was delicious, frosting clinging to my teeth, making the taste last longer. I didn't stop until my plate was empty, until I had gobbled up every last crumb. Only then did I look up at my brother, realizing he hadn't touched his cake yet.

"What's the matter?" I asked him. "Why won't you eat your cake? Is your tummy sore again?"

He didn't respond. It didn't even seem like he heard me. All he did was sit there, staring at our mother, his eyes hard and cold. I had never seen him like this, and it scared me a little, killing one excited butterfly after the other.

"Glenn—" I started when the front door opened, voices carried in with the winter chill. "Dad!" I jumped off the chair and rushed to the front door, greeting him with the biggest smile, slapping my arms around his waist as I hugged him. "Dad, you have to taste the cake Mommy baked. It's the best cake ever."

He smiled, brushing his hands through my hair. "I'm sure it is. No one bakes a better cake than your mom."

"Come on." I grabbed his hand, not the least bit curious about the present Mom said he would bring me. I just wanted him to have a slice of the cake, and maybe then Mom would let me have another one.

"Hold on, sweetheart." Dad pulled me back to him. "I want you to meet my friend." I turned, and only then did I notice the man who stood next to him. It was a young man, younger than Dad. Dark hair, dark eyes, and a smile as warm as a summer breeze.

"You must be the birthday girl." He crouched down. "My name is Jeffrey."

I tightened my hold on Dad's hand. "I'm Dahlia."

"That is such a pretty name." His dark eyes turned black, and I didn't like the way he stared at me.

"Jeffrey is here to celebrate with us." Dad picked me up, and I chuckled. "It's not every day that my little girl turns ten. Double digits."

"Why is he here?"

All of us turned toward Glenn, who stood by the entrance to the dining room.

"Like I just said," Dad replied. "To help celebrate Dahlia's birthday."

"That's not why he's here, is it?" I noticed his fists balled at his sides, his glare solely focused on Jeffrey.

"Of course it is."

"No, it's not." Glenn's jaw clenched, his eyebrows knitted together.

Dad put me down before straightening again. "Do not be rude to our guest, son."

I didn't like the way Dad's voice went from warm and welcoming to cold and hard. More butterflies died.

"Come on, Glenn. I think you should go to your room for a bit." Mom placed her hands on his shoulders, but he jerked away.

"Don't touch me!"

"Glenn," she scolded. "You're embarrassing us. Stop it."

"No. Why is he here? Why did Dad bring a stranger home? What is he doing here?" he shouted. "He has to leave. This is Dahlia's birthday. He has to leave!"

Glenn was so angry, and he kept screaming and screaming. Mom tried to reach for his arm when he grabbed the long sleeve of her red dress, tearing it right off.

I gasped. Mom's pretty red dress was ruined, and her smile was gone. *No. No. No.* I wanted her to smile again. It was my birthday. *Please smile.*

"It's for your medicine, isn't it?" Glenn threw the torn sleeve to the floor. "He's here to hurt Dahlia so you can get your medicine. I won't let you hurt Dahlia. I won't let you hurt her." Tears streamed down his face, but his eyes were still hard, jaw still set.

Dad grabbed him, lifting his feet off the ground while Glenn kept kicking and screaming.

"I won't let you hurt her. You won't hurt my little sister!"

"Glenn, please." I started crying. "Stop it!"

I rushed to the corner, all the butterflies gone. Dead. Forgotten.

I closed my eyes, Glenn's screams mixed with Dad's curses making my tummy ache.

"Leave her alone! Don't hurt her! I'll kill you. I'll kill all of you!" Glenn screamed, and then there was a loud *thwack*, a sound that cracked through the house. When I opened my eyes, Glenn was on the floor, eyes closed like he was sleeping. There was a smear of blood at the corner of his mouth, and I choked on a breath when I realized Dad had hit him.

Mom was crying as Dad picked his seemingly lifeless body from the floor, carrying him up the stairs.

I looked at Jeffrey, who still stood by the front door, hands tucked in his pants pockets, a slight smirk on his face as he watched everything that was happening. He didn't seem frightened at all—not the way I was.

Mom clutched her naked arm, and I noticed the blue and yellow bruises on the inside of her elbow. She wiped away the tears, pulled her palms down her dress, and wiped some strands of hair from her face.

"I'm sorry about that, Jeffrey. Please, come have a piece of cake."

He smiled at her. "No problem at all. Kids will be kids." When he turned to face me, I shivered.

"Come on, Dahlia," Mom urged, holding out her hand. "I think you should have another slice of cake. How does that sound?"

I shook my head, Glenn's cries still echoing in my head.

Not even another piece of cake would be able to bring the butterflies back to life.

"Come on." She held out her hand, and with hesitant steps, I moved out of the corner, biting my lip, my cheeks still wet from crying. My birthday was ruined. Glenn ruined my birthday by misbehaving and being rude to Daddy's friend. It was all his fault that my butterflies disappeared.

It was all his fault.

I sat down at the dining table and watched silently as Mom cut more cake. Jeffrey took a seat next to me, placing a brown paper bag on the table. "This cake looks delicious. I think we should have something to drink with the cake, don't you?" He smiled at me, reaching out, gently tucking my hair behind my ear. I didn't like the way it felt when he touched me.

From the corner of my eye, I saw Mom take the paper bag, peeking inside. She closed her eyes, taking a deep breath, almost like she smelled something she liked. Something wasn't right. I felt it in my chest, the way my heart raced, willing me to run. Why did Glenn think Jeffrey was here to hurt me?

Mom closed the bag. "I'll go pour us something to drink." She walked to the kitchen, and a part of me didn't want to be left alone with Daddy's friend. But I knew better than to call out after her, to beg her not to leave me alone here.

I placed my hands in my lap, staring down at the slice of cake in front of me, no longer craving its sugary sweetness.

"What's the matter, Dahlia? You don't like the cake?" He placed his hand on my leg, his long fingers wrapping around my knee. It felt wrong, the way he touched me. But I didn't move. I couldn't. I didn't want Daddy's friend to think I was rude.

He shifted his seat closer. "Would you like me to feed you?"

I shook my head, and his hand crept higher up my leg.

"You look real pretty in that dress." I swallowed while I felt his fingers slither up the inside of my thigh. "The purple color brings out the blue in your eyes."

I bit my lip, willing the burning tears away. Mom came back into the living room, and I exhaled, relieved that she was back and I was no longer alone with Daddy's friend. But Jeffrey didn't take his hand off my leg. He thanked my mother for the drinks then pushed my glass closer toward me.

My mom smiled at me, but this time I didn't like her smile.

"Drink up, sweetheart. When you're done with your drink, you're getting your present."

I no longer wanted the present. The butterflies died. There was no more excitement for birthday parties, cake, or presents.

"Drink up, Dahlia," Jeffrey urged, his fingers drawing circles on my leg, my skin burning.

I swallowed, my throat dry, my heart racing faster than it ever did before. My tummy felt heavy, achy, my arms and legs trembling. Something wasn't right. The sweat beading at the back of my neck warned me that something wasn't right.

My mom.

My dad.

Glenn.

Jeffrey.

The brown paper bag.

Something wasn't right.

"He's here to hurt Dahlia so you can get your medicine. I won't let you hurt Dahlia. I won't let you hurt her."

Jeffrey leaned closer, and I felt his warm breath against my cheek. I didn't want him to come any closer, so I reached for the drink as a distraction, a way to get just a little distance from the man who still had his hand on my leg.

The soda tasted different, a little bitterness mixed with the sweet. The bubbles burned my throat as I swallowed, but I drank it all. Every last drop.

"Such a good girl," Jeffrey uttered, his words sharp like knives. He *was* here to hurt me. Glenn was right. Daddy's friend came here to hurt me.

He reached out, touching my chin and turning my face to his. But I didn't look at him, keeping my eyes on the untouched slice of chocolate cake.

"Your daddy was right. You are the prettiest little girl in town."

My heart hiccupped, my body numb. I didn't know what to do. I wanted him to stop touching me, but I didn't want to make Mommy and Daddy angry. I didn't want to be punished again, locked in my room for days, having to pee on the floor. And I didn't want Daddy to hit me the way he hit Glenn. But I wanted Jeffrey to stop touching me, and to leave.

What do I do?

What do I do?

Jeffrey traced his nose across my jaw, and his breathing started to deepen. "You smell just as sweet as the cake." His hand slipped under my dress, fingers brushing against my panties.

It hurt. But not where he touched me. It hurt inside my chest. It hurt there where my heart pounded.

I looked up at Mommy, pleading at her with my gaze to

make him stop. But she simply smiled, her eyes hooded and heavy. She had the same look on her face whenever she took her medicine, like she somehow managed to escape this world—like she was flying high, far away from us. Away from me.

When I felt him slip his fingers through the side of my panties, I jumped up. But as my feet hit the ground, I tripped, the world suddenly turning, spinning faster and faster. My head felt strange, and I blinked as my vision blurred.

What's happening?

I tried to get up. I tried to reach for my mom, but she moved farther and farther away from me, even though she just stood there leaning against the entryway.

"Mommy—"

"It's okay, Dahlia," I heard her say. "You're going to get your present now. A present only meant for big girls...like you."

I closed my eyes, dizziness making me feel sick. My stomach turned, and my arms and legs became numb. I didn't know what was happening. All I knew was I wanted the butterflies back. I wanted to feel their wings flutter with excitement again, like they did before Daddy came home. But they never came back.

Ever.

Present

FTER MIDDAY, and I refused to leave my bedroom. I
nted to stay there and sulk like a little bitch, feeling
for myself. It had been a while since I allowed myself a
party. Seemed like Onyx changed a lot of things for me.

First, he managed to make me find pleasure in a man's
uch, then proved to me that I wasn't just an object whose
only worth was to get fucked. He showed me what it was like
to be made love to, to be worshipped between the sheets
instead of used against walls and tables.

His touch. His kiss. The affection he showed me, it was
incredible yet startling at the same time. For as long as I
could remember, my brother was the only person who ever
cared for me—at least that was what I thought, what I had
believed my whole life.

No man had ever treated me like something precious.
But Onyx did. In his bed, he treated me like a queen,
refusing to use me the way I was used to. Now I wasn't sure

whether I'd be able to go back to my old life afte
after finally experiencing how it was supposed to be.

Turning on my side, I exhaled, nestling my head
into my pillow. After Slither left my room, I dragg
confused and tired ass to my bed, and I stayed there f
last few hours. Slither wanted me to do another job for
the kind of job that had always been my way of paying
back for taking care of me. The first few times he had
entertain some of his VIPs, I would throw up afterward
shower under scorching hot water until my skin turn
crimson. But eventually, the self-loathing that came with t
dirty deeds disappeared, replaced with a sense of duty. Th
jobs became easier, and I started playing the game like
pro, but I never got to a point where I was able to enjoy a
single minute of it. Every touch, every kiss, every thrust felt
vile, like a piece of my soul died every single time.

But not with him. Not with Onyx. And it confused the
hell out of me. Why would something that had always felt
shameful and abhorrent turn into something that felt
amazing and beautiful simply because it was him touching
me, kissing me, thrusting into me?

A tear slipped down my cheek and lapped onto the
pillowcase. It had been a years since I found myself in this
hole—a pit where nothing but darkness lurked. Yet all I
could think about was how much I wanted to be with him
again. How I longed to look into his striking blue eyes, hear
his voice, feel his touch. Every fiber in my being urged me to
go to him, to be with him...just one last time, without someone's vendetta and orders forcing me to. But the question
was, would I survive it? Would I be able to be with him
without breaking, without giving away my true self?

Turning on my back, I stared up at the ceiling, tears
escaping down the sides of my face. I closed my eyes, trying

to imagine his face, but the image in my head didn't do him justice. It only made me want to see him so much more.

"Ugh," I sighed. "Fuck this." I shot up and grabbed my boots, slipping them on before grabbing my jacket, revealing the knife beneath it. His knife. The knife I stole from him, replacing it with mine. I bit my lip as I eased a fingertip over the steel. Just this once, I wanted to do something I wanted to do, something my heart begged me to do.

Just. This. Once.

~

Onyx

I GLANCED at the clock on the wall. It was just past noon, a good enough time for me to grab an ice-cold beer from the fridge, cracking the lid and taking a large gulp.

Ink was pissed at me, and rightfully so. I understood why he felt the way he did, but my decisions no longer affected me alone, which was why I had to think with my head—make the best decision based on facts and not personal opinions.

Leaning against the wall, my mind wandered to the woman whose perfume still lingered on my pillowcases. Wraith. I had to admit, even though I was disappointed at her disappearance, I wasn't surprised. She didn't seem like the type who stuck around for pillow talk and romantic morning-afters. But, damn, there was a very big part of me that wished I had either cuffed her to my bed, or locked her in my goddamn room because I really fucking wanted to see her right now. And like Granite said, I didn't have her number or know where she stayed. All I had was the memories of how her body felt against mine, how she surrendered, letting go of her demons only for a little while as I showed her what it was like to be taken by a man determined to give her pleasure rather than take it.

"Fuck," I muttered, pushing myself off the wall on my way to the stairs. That was when I heard it, the sound of a Harley out front. Immediately, my heart started to pound like a jackhammer, hoping like fuck it was her. I knew it wasn't trouble heading our way since trouble didn't come with a single engine.

Rushing to the door, I flung it open and stared right at her. I exhaled as I took her in. With dark circles under her eyes and splotchy complexion, she looked exhausted. Troubled. "You had me worried. I didn't know whether you'd come back."

"To be honest, I wasn't sure whether I would."

Unable to stop myself, I reached out and grabbed her wrist, pulling her inside the bar and slamming the door shut as I pressed her back against it. I didn't know what it was, but whenever I was near her, I turned into this possessive fucker who would do anything to keep her, to make sure no one else touched her.

I slipped my finger down her chin, settling it in the hollow below her throat. "Why do you keep running from me?"

"I'm trying to save you."

"From what?"

Her plump lips parted. "Me."

I smirked. "You know, for a man like me, that's not a warning. It's a fucking challenge." I gripped her chin between my fingers, puckering those sweet lips of hers right before I kissed her so fucking hard we both groaned like hungry beasts. I didn't care about her forewarning. As a matter of fact, she could have told me she was the daughter of Satan, and I'd still want her like I'd never wanted any other woman before. Our lips devoured, our moans collided, and our kiss fucking shattered every ounce of resistance. My mind, my body, my fucking soul were all invested in that one goddamn kiss. A kiss powerful enough to bring even a mean motherfucker like me to my knees.

Reluctantly, I peeled my lips from hers but kept them a mere breath apart. "Stop running from me, Dahlia."

Her lips were red and swollen, her eyes desperate and hooded. "It's not that simple, Onyx."

"Yes, it is," I breathed out. "It is that simple. Everything in life is fucking simple. It's us who choose to complicate shit. And right now, you're complicating it by overthinking what's happening between us."

"It's not—"

I placed my thumb over her red lips, smothering her words. "I know it feels insane, and it's crazy, but by God, it feels so fucking right." I pulled back an inch, looking her square in the eye. "Tell me you don't feel it too? Tell me you don't feel how fucking right this is?"

The way she bit her lip, her eyes gleaming as she stared back at me, I knew she couldn't. There was no way in hell she could have been able to deny that there was this wild, powerful pull between us. A chemistry that was too damn powerful to ignore.

"Dahlia, I know you have demons chasing you. We all do." I placed my hand on her chest, slowly tracing a fingertip between her breasts, pulling her shirt down the middle to reveal the lotus flower inked on her skin. "But like the lotus flower, you can submerge yourself into the dirtiest, darkest corners of this world and stay there for however long. But when you're with me, you turn into this beautiful creature—unblemished, unscarred, and just fucking perfect. Last night proved that."

"Onyx," she reached out, placing a palm on my cheek, "God knows, I want to be with you. I really do."

"Then be. Don't run from me."

Licking her lips, she pulled her hand away from my face, diverting her eyes. Whatever it was that kept her from staying with me was slowly starting to infect our time together, and there was no way in hell I would let her run from me. Not now. I needed her to open up and tell me who or what these demons were that refused to let her be with me.

"Come on." I grabbed her wrist.

"Where are we going?"

"Just come with me." I walked outside to my hog. "Get on."

"What?"

"Get on. I want to take you for a ride."

She pursed her lips and crossed her arms. "Do I look like fender fluff?"

I snickered. "Just get the fuck on, would you?"

Her eyes narrowed, brows slanted inward. "Fine."

I was sure I had a grin the size of Japan on my face. Climbing on my hog, I waited for her to get on behind me before I started the engine. The second she wrapped her arms around me, I could swear to God I felt my entire universe shift, like something just fucking clicked in place. I wasn't a unicorns and rainbows kind of guy, and I always believed fate was for pussies. But this moment right here was powerful enough to make a man like me hope like fuck there was such a thing as fate, and that her name was engraved into mine.

"Where you taking me?" She leaned her head on my shoulder.

"You just hold on tight, buttercup."

Revving the engine, I pulled onto the street and burned rubber. I knew Wraith wouldn't have a problem with speeding, so I didn't hold back. That was one of the things I loved about being with her—she had the same wild spirit I did.

We kept riding for miles, and she didn't loosen her grip around my waist once. This felt so right, having her on my hog, her arms around me, her breath in my neck. I didn't want the ride to stop, wishing it could last forever.

Slowing down, I pulled to the side of the road, next to a view of Brighton Beach, and switched off the ignition.

"What are we doing here?" She moved her arms as she tried to get off, but I grabbed her wrist, keeping it place.

"I come here whenever shit gets too much. You know, just to breathe."

She didn't say anything as she rested her chin in my shoulder, staring at the view in front of us.

"Tell me."

Her thighs shifted beside me. "Tell you what?"

"Tell me who hurt you. Tell me your secrets."

For the longest time, we just sat there, her breathing mixing with the sound of the waves. I didn't let go of her wrist, making sure she didn't remove her arms from around me.

She sighed against my neck. "My world is dark, Onyx."

"So is mine."

"I'm not talking about crews, or clubs, or gun wars. I'm talking about my life."

I tightened my grip around her wrist. "You connected with Neon last night. I saw it. I saw the way you looked at her. It was like you felt her pain."

"I did. I still feel it."

I brought her hand up to my mouth, placing a kiss on the top of her hand. "Tell me your secrets, Dahlia Knight."

"I don't want you to carry that burden as well."

"It's not up to you to decide which burdens I carry and which I don't."

"Onyx," she nestled her face into my back, and I felt her tightening her arms around me, "I'm poison."

"I don't care. In fact, I don't give a fuck how toxic you think you are. I want you, and I will go on a rampage through hell if that means I can have you."

I looked out over the ocean, the sun high in the sky, the ripples in the waves shimmering like millions of diamonds.

"Someone in my past hurt me," she started. "Hurt me real bad."

My chest ached, rage starting to bubble up to the surface.

"It hurt me in such a way that I was never able to handle a man's touch...not until you."

My ribs cracked, and every hair on my body stood up. "Who?" I gritted out.

"It doesn't matter. They don't exist anymore."

"They?" I pinched my eyes closed, desperate to not lose my shit. She was opening up because I pushed her to. If I lost it now, she'd never tell me anything again.

I felt her chest expand against my back as she took a deep breath. "Yeah...they."

"So, they're dead?"

"Yeah."

"Did you—"

"No. No, I didn't." She paused, and it was like a heavy cloud settled over us even though the sun was burning down the summer heat. "But my brother did."

16

WRAITH

I took a few seconds to process what she just told me. She didn't have to spit it out word for word for me to know how she was hurt. I also knew there were so much more to her past, but I wouldn't push any more today. At least I got something—a puzzle piece toward solving the secrets she kept buried.

I let go of her wrist and held her arm as she climbed off the bike. I got off too and reached for her, pulling her closer and settling my hand on her hip. "Listen to me very carefully." I looked her dead in the eye. "I don't give a flying fuck about your past. You got that?"

Radiant irises stared at me, unshed tears shimmering in the corners. "I told you, I'll only ruin you."

"I don't care."

"But I do." She placed her palms against my chest, fingers sliding down my cut. "I care about you, Onyx. Too much. And what you have with your crew—"

"Listen, I know all this club business can be really shitty at times, but I can be a president of a crew and still be your man."

A pretty pink blush spread across her cheeks, and her complexion turned to a healthy glow under the summer sun. "It's too risky."

"Why?"

She bit her lip, her attention dropping to where her hands touched my chest.

"Wraith, I'll do everything in my fucking power to protect you. I know being with me comes with a shitload of risks, but I swear to God there is no man strong enough to take you from me."

"You hardly know me."

"I don't care. All that matters is that I know I want you. There's no guarantees, I know that." I tucked a stray strand of her hair behind her ear. "But I think if we don't stick around to see where this is heading, we'd regret it."

She closed her eyes, and I could feel her hesitation roll off her in waves of confusion.

When she opened her eyes, her irises were swirling with uncertainty, beautiful lips pulled in a straight line. "I'll only hurt you," she said, like she already regretted it.

I shook my head. "You don't know that."

"Yes. I do."

"I'm a big boy, Wraith. I'll risk it."

"Why? Would you want to risk anything where I'm concerned?"

"Because I would rather have you for a moment to realize it won't work than not have you at all and always wonder what if," I placed my palms on her cheeks, "what if it would have worked."

With parted lips she stared up at me. "You're the president of the American Street Kings. A crew—"

"—which you'll have no problem fitting in to."

"Onyx—"

"Wraith, stop looking for excuses not to jump into the deep end with me. Just go with it. Stop running and just be with me. No promises, no guarantees." I pulled her closer, her body flush against mine, the summer breeze wafting raven strands into her face. "One day at a time, that's all I'm asking."

Her lips pursed as she chewed the inside of her cheek, and I practically heard the wheels turn inside her head. Pushing herself up on her toes, she placed a gentle kiss against my lips, her mouth lingering on mine, our breaths colliding. Jesus Christ, I had never experienced this before. I had never wanted a woman as much as I wanted her. It was like our souls were connected, and the thought of not being with her, of not having her was powerful enough to fuck with my head in the worst possible way.

My lips ached when she pulled away, desperate for more of her taste. And as our gazes met, she smiled, but it didn't reach her eyes. "You're a good man, Onyx. I can see why she cares for you."

"Who?"

"Alyx."

I cocked a brow. "What the fuck does Alyx have to do with this?"

"Nothing," she shook her head lightly, "she just made it clear that she didn't want you to get hurt."

"What? Why—"

"Calm down. She was subtle about it, and I get it. I get that you're all like family, something I've never had."

"Wraith, I know you've been hurt. I know there's demons in your past, but don't let it keep you away from me."

She stepped back a little, and I hated the distance between us. "Just...take me back. Please."

"Wraith, don't. You're pulling away again." I reached for her, but she moved out of my reach, like she was afraid I'd burn her.

"I need time."

Instantly, hope flared. Those words were better than a fucking no. "Okay." I placed my hands on my hips, staring at her with intent. "Just know that if you disappear on me, I will look for you. And I won't stop until I've found you. You hear me?" I stepped up to her and grabbed her chin between my fingers, lifting her face to mine. "I will turn this city upside down for you, woman. I swear to God."

17

WRAITH

I WENT STRAIGHT HOME—TO the Python clubhouse after the ride I took with Onyx. My head was a mess, my heart in chaos. Every second I spent with him I felt him claw his way deeper into my heart. He was so sure I was the woman he wanted. But he didn't know me—know who I really was. Everything he thought he knew was a lie. A lie that started the very first second he laid eyes on me. And on my way back home, his every word echoing in my mind, I was convinced that the certainty in his eyes was just a ripple effect of me pretending to be someone I wasn't.

Even though it physically hurt to walk through the halls of my brother's compound, knowing my life was nothing but a giant hole of nothing, I was smart enough to realize that it would never change. My life would never change. There was no hope for Onyx and me, because he would never accept me if I had to tell him the truth. And I could no longer live this lie. I could no longer look into his eyes, see the affection he felt for me reflect in his irises without me feeling a gut-wrenching guilt strong enough to tear me apart.

So, this was it. I had no choice but to move on—away

and without Onyx, a man I had been deceiving since the very beginning. This was my life, and the sooner I made peace with it, the better. And after I got this job done for Slither tonight, I planned on telling him that I would no longer be his spy on the fucking Kings. I would do all his other jobs forever and a day—but not the Kings. Not Onyx.

Never again.

The red dress I wore was way too tight. But Glenn—or rather, Slither—insisted I wear it. Said red was this guy's favorite color, and the tighter, the better. In the past, I didn't give situations like these a second thought. It was part of my life, part of me paying my way around here. My way of *contributing* to the crew. Slither didn't want me riding with them as a crew member, said women weren't allowed to wear the Python patch. And he definitely didn't want me being fender fluff since, well...I was his sister. Everyone around here knew they'd be as good as dead if they touched me. If they didn't believe it, they were more than welcome to ask the corpse currently serving as fish bait at the bottom of the ocean—the body of a man whose throat Slither cut because he thought my ass was fair game for crew members. Needless to say, no other man here even looked my way after that. I was like the local leprosy patient with everyone walking circles around me. But it didn't bother me. The less I had to deal with guys walking around with their dicks on their foreheads, the better. And my *job* here didn't bother me either...until today. For the last ten years, I had been too grateful for what Slither had done for me to doubt my place here. If fucking clients, VIPs to the Pythons, or anyone Slither needed money, business, or information from was what it took to show my gratitude and loyalty, I did it. It still didn't compensate for what my brother had done for me all those years ago. But today, I struggled. I struggled to put my game face on, to get my head in the right space to do what needed to be done. With every click of my heel against the concrete, doubt dug its claws deeper into my mind. I tried to focus on the profile Slither had given me. The man I was supposed to impress enough to ensure he didn't take his business elsewhere. According to my brother, this man was the most important client the Pythons had ever had, and my performance tonight better be a game changer. With my dark hair straightened and heavy make-up illuminating my skin and lengthening my eyelashes, I was hardly recognizable as the Wraith everyone knew.

Slither waited by the door, his smile stretching from ear to ear. His split tongue and snakelike appearance never bothered me. To the world, it was a man trying to be a monster—a freak who wanted to look as ugly on the outside as he was on the inside. But I knew what the motivation was behind every tattooed scale, and the tongue torn in two.

"You look gorgeous, little sister."

I smiled. "Thanks." I glanced at the club door and up to the neon pink sign that read 'Jitters.'

I cocked a brow at my brother. "A strip club?"

"The Sixes own it."

"Of course they do," I muttered and rolled my eyes.

Slither grabbed my elbow and pulled me close, fingers digging into my flesh. "You better behave tonight, little sis. Or I swear to God I'll—"

"I always behave," I bit out before he could finish his threat. One thing about words, they could never be taken back. I didn't want Slither to go there, to say something that would wreck us. He was all I had left in this world.

Whiskey eyes lingered on mine, his hand gripping my elbow loosening slightly, a gentle fingertip tracing circles on my skin. "You look just like her."

"Don't say that."

"It's true. You're just as beautiful as she was."

I jerked my arm from his grasp, ice smothering the blood in my veins. "Why are you saying this?"

"Because it's true." He smiled. "I dreamt of her the other night, and when I woke up, I realized you look just like her."

"Stop." Unease crawled all over my skin. I didn't like the look in his eyes while he talked about her, comparing me to her.

Slither pulled a palm over his tattooed head and took a breath like he had to take a second to pull his shit together. "You better not fuck this up. If you ever had to impress anyone, this guy is it. You need to pull out all the stops tonight, do you understand? Don't disappoint me."

I nodded, trying my best not to show how conflicted I was. The last thing I needed was for Slither to think I was doubting my own loyalty to him. Especially after what the Kings claimed my brother did to Neon—the woman whose screams shook the early hours of this morning. The things Onyx said they did to her, I couldn't believe it was my brother. Not Glenn.

But maybe Slither?

I knew there was a darkness in him. I carried that same darkness. But I was sure we were both strong enough not to let it consume us, and that we could control it enough for it to numb the pain of the past and make sure nothing hurt us ever again.

I shifted from one leg to the other, the summer breeze caressing my legs with its warm fingers. "At least tell me why this Crow guy is so important to you."

"To us," he corrected. "Important to us. The Sixes have more money than you can imagine. Their connections go straight into the motherfucking White House. If we want someone on our side, we want the Sixes."

"What business do we have with them?"

Slither *tsk'd*. "Dear sister, you know better than to ask me that."

Yeah. I did know better. He never discussed club business with me, only giving me information I needed, like the profile he gave me of Crow.

Cassian "Crow" Blackwood. President of the Sixes for the last eleven years.

Killing was as easy as breathing for this man, running his empire with an iron fist. As far as bad guys went, this man was the worst.

Sexual tastes? Hardcore.

Hard limits? He was the fucking hard limit.

A simple blowjob or quick fuck wasn't going to cut it with this guy. If I wanted to impress him the way Slither wanted me to, I had to bring my A-game and show no fear. Only confidence. Complete submission.

"Here they come." Slither turned, and I heard the roaring engines of their Ducatis in the distance. Unlike other crews around here the Sixes were all about speed and burning rubber. To be part of their crew your ride had to be a black Ducati, and nothing else. Whenever they went on a run, they looked like a sea of black, speeding past in a blur of velocity. With sweaty palms and a racing heart, I watched as they rode toward us.

"Shut it off," Slither started, glancing my way, "just like I taught you."

I nodded. "Just like you taught me."

BLOOD STAINED *the white sheets draped over my bed. My dress* was torn and smeared with red too. I had woken up on the filthy bedding, my head aching along with the rest of my body. I felt groggy, weak, like I had eaten spoiled food again. But the blood? I wasn't sure where it came from. Why did it hurt down there?

I couldn't sit up, so I remained on my side, tears streaming down my face turning the white sheets a light shade of gray with every drop. It was too sore to move, and I tried to call someone, but the words wouldn't form inside my head. It wouldn't come out.

I had no idea how I ended up in my room. The last thing I remembered was being in the dining room, staring at my second slice of cake. But I didn't eat it...because he was there. Daddy's friend. The man who killed the butterflies.

A sharp pain jabbed between my thighs, shooting up my tummy. It burned everywhere, like the night Mommy's cigarette burned the top of my hand. Only this was a thousand times worse. Like a thousand of Mommy's cigarettes were burning all over my body, all at once.

I clutched my tummy and cried into the pillow. I didn't know what happened to me, why I was so sore, but I knew it was something wrong. This wasn't how a big girl was supposed to feel. I wasn't supposed to bleed there.

I had no memories of what happened, but the longer I lay there, the more images started to flash before my eyes.

His face.

His eyes.

His hands.

The noises he made.

It was wrong.

Everything was wrong, and I wanted it to stop. I'd rather not remember.

"Dahlia?"

For a moment, I didn't recognize his voice.

"Dahlia, it's Glenn."

I felt him place his hand on my ankle, and I didn't know why, but the second he touched me, I jerked away, scrambling with my achy body to the top of the bed. Away from him. Away from someone touching me.

"Dahlia. I won't hurt you. Please."

I pushed my face deeper into the pillow, my breathing fast and out of control, like I had just run all the way home from school.

"Dahlia, let me help you."

I wiped the tears away, looking at my brother standing next to my bed. "He hurt me." Finally, I managed to say something.

"I know." A tear slowly slipped down his cheek, and he crouched beside me, his eyes level with mine.

"Did he hurt you too?"

He shook his head. "No."

I sniffed, wiping at my nose.

"But Dad's other friends...they hurt me."

"Why?" I didn't understand why they would want to hurt us.

"Because they're bad people."

I placed my chin on the pillow, looking at my brother. "That's why you didn't smile."

He stared back at me, more tears running down his cheeks, a big blue bruise protruding from the side of his face.

"You didn't smile because you knew Daddy's friend would hurt me. That's why you didn't eat your cake."

The mattress dipped, and Glenn got on the bed with me, lying down on top of the bloodstains, hiding it. I liked that he could take it away.

He took my hand while he kept looking at me. "You know what I do when they start hurting me?"

I shook my head.

"I use my superpower."

"You don't have a superpower, silly."

He smiled. "I do. I turn into a snake."

"A snake?"

He nodded. "A snake can shed its skin. That's what I do when they come for me. I shed my skin and slither away so they can't hurt me."

I swallowed, my mouth feeling dry. "How?"

His thumb drew lazy circles on my hand. "By closing my eyes, and then I imagine it."

"Imagining you have a superpower doesn't count," I protested.

"Of course it does. If you imagine something hard enough, it can really happen."

I watched our hands joined together. "Where do you go... when you slither away?"

"Somewhere they can't find me. But you're there."

"I am?" I couldn't help but smile. I liked that he took me with him whenever he used his superpower to get away from the bad people.

He smiled back at me, but just like when we had cake, his smile didn't reach his eyes. "I'll always take you with me, no matter where I go."

That made me feel better. It stilled the pain a bit, knowing he would never leave me behind. But then I realized what he was really saying.

"Mom and Dad are going to bring more bad people here... aren't they?"

His smile faltered, replaced with hard lines. "Yes, Dahlia. They are."

"I wish I had a superpower that can make me go back in time."

"Yeah," he said softy, "then you can make it so this never happened."

I shook my head, biting the inside of my cheek. "No. I would go back in time to make a different wish when I blow out my birthday candles."

His eyes glimmered with tears. "What did you wish for?"

"I wished that I'd have a birthday like this one every year." I closed my eyes. "But I don't want that anymore. I want to wish that this birthday never happened."

"Don't," he warned with a hard yet soft voice. "Don't ever allow yourself to go back and imagine how things could have been. It only makes it worse. Just..." He swallowed. "Just turn into a snake. Slither away, and only come back once the bad people are gone."

"I can't," I cried. "I'm not as strong as you. I don't have a superpower."

"Then you turn it off. You hear me?" He let go of my hand, placing his palm on my cheek. "Then you turn your mind off, shut it all down. Don't feel. Don't hear. And don't think. Be a void. Be nothing. In those moments, be. Nothing. Can you do that?"

I pinched my eyes closed as tears now ran uncontrollably down my cheeks.

"Dahlia, look at me."

I opened my eyes, his face blurry.

"Can you do that? Please, promise me you'll do that every time you're forced to do something you don't want to do. Shut it. Off."

There was only enough strength left in me to give a slight nod. I was suddenly tired, my eyes heavy and body weak.

"Glenn?"

"Yeah?"

I smiled sleepily. "I'm glad you didn't eat cake."

"Why is that?"

"Because then Daddy's friend would have hurt you too."

Silence. He didn't say anything, and I was too weak to talk any more. I just wanted the darkness to take me, because the *farther I slipped into the void, the nothingness Glenn had told me about, the more the pain dissipated.*

I felt his hand brush against my cheek. "Sleep, little sis. I'll be here when you wake up."

"Promise?"

"I promise."

I wiped my nose on the pillow before nestling deeper into it. Sleep was lessening the pain—not just the pain between my legs, but the pain in my chest too.

"I'm sorry." *He sighed, and I managed to open my eyes in time to see a tear slip between his lips.* "I'm sorry I couldn't stop them."

I closed my eyes again.

"But I promise, when I'm big enough, I'll stop them. And then no one will ever hurt you again. Do you believe me?"

I simply nodded, my cheeks rubbing against the rough fabric of my pillow.

"Dahlia, say you believe me."

"I believe you," *I whispered.* "I believe you."

The butterflies never came back after that day. And neither did I.

It was easy to spot Crow among the rest of the crew. He was the biggest, meanest looking motherfucker in the front. Arrogance and power clung to him like a second skin, his superiority easily spotted. Sleek, long hair, the color of midnight, hung down his back between his shoulder blades in a low-tied ponytail. His beard was as dark as his hair, his cheeks cleanly shaven, leaving a thick chin strap along his jawline. When he got off his hog, I stopped breathing as I watched him straighten his big frame.

Slither wasn't kidding when he said this man was the

worst of the bad. It radiated off him, the malice and wickedness.

Wearing faded black jeans, leather cut, and black shirt, he oozed more power than any Wall Street suit.

I swallowed hard, the mere sight of him intimidating me, letting my confidence falter. And all I could think about was Onyx, seeing his face, feeling his touch. How good it felt to be with him. "Slither," I turned to him, "I can't do this."

"Yes, you can. And you fucking will."

I shook my head. "Don't make me do this, please."

"Do not start this fucking bullshit," he gritted between clenched teeth. "You are doing this, or I swear to fucking God, I will hurt you more than anyone has ever hurt you before."

I stumbled back, his words hitting me square in the chest. If there ever was someone who knew how badly I had been hurt before in my life, it was him. For him to threaten to hurt me worse than that...it was horrifying.

"Glenn, what's gotten into you?"

He moved in front of me, blocking me from the Sixes. Angry eyes glared at me with a kind of hate that crawled all the way up my spine. "I fucking warned you not to call me that." He grabbed my wrist, twisting it up between us, pressing our bodies against each other.

"You're hurting me."

"You're testing my patience, little sister. I swear to motherfucking God, if you don't do this job, I'm going to hurt you so much more than this."

I lifted my chin in defiance. "Who are you? Because you sure as hell ain't my brother anymore."

"That's right." He tightened his grip, leaning down, stoning me with his whispered words. "Right now, I'm your fucking God, and you will do as I say."

He let go of me, gently easing back, making sure no one witnessed the animosity that pulsed like a heartbeat between us.

"Now pull your shit together and get your head in the game."

I glanced at him, the warning clear in his eyes. Disappoint him, and I would regret it.

Slither's men rounded us as he approached Crow. I couldn't hear what they were saying as they leaned close together. Slither always made sure I was never on the hearing end of any of his business conversations. But he didn't know I was on the hearing end back at the Kings' compound, hearing things about a man I didn't know. A man who was supposedly my brother, yet...I hardly recognized him anymore. It became all the more clear that the man before me now was no longer the boy who swore to protect me, but rather a power-hungry, cruel, and vindictive monster who thrived on the pain of others.

Slither waved me over, and I steeled myself, draping a veil of fake confidence over my shoulders. I walked toward them, sashaying my hips and crossing my feet like I fucking owned every step. Clutching my purse and flicking my hair over my shoulder, I pulled on my game face.

"Crow, meet Wraith. One of my girls." He looked me in the eye. "But tonight...she's your girl."

18

ONYX

"GOD, I HATE THESE MOTHERFUCKING CAGES," Manic complained, shifting uncomfortably in his seat. "Why are we here, again?"

I stared out the window at the neon sign illuminated against the night sky. "If Dutch's info is correct, Slither will have to distract Crow tonight if he wants his shipment to come in without the Sixes getting eyes on it."

"Still don't get why we're on the outside of a goddamn strip club, and not on the inside."

"It's called a stakeout, you dumb fuck. If we're in there, we might as well call it a suicide."

"Dying among bare titties sounds like a good way to go to me."

I scowled at him, not even sure that remark deserved any type of response. "Shut up and keep your eyes peeled, okay?"

"Fine. It just feels wrong to sit here while there are two dozen naked girls on the inside of that building. You know," he held up a hand, "I bet if Ink were here, we'd be tucking

Benjamins into teeny-tiny little thongs right about now. He's always been the fun one."

"Yeah, well, I don't think that Ink exists anymore."

To say Ink was pissed at me for leaving him behind was an understatement. But the way his anger started to control him more and more, I wasn't sure I could trust him to keep it together. Right now, we couldn't afford any mistakes. I couldn't chance it.

"Hey," Manic pointed to the door, "isn't that Slither?"

I narrowed my eyes, staring at the figure in the distance. "Yeah, that's him. The ugly fuck." That was a face I could recognize a mile away.

A car stopped in front of the building, and I pulled out my phone to take some images.

"Who's the girl?" Manic asked, both of us watching as a woman in a red mini dress approached him, her back toward us.

"I have no idea."

Manic whistled in appreciation. "Look at those mother-fucking fine legs."

I just rolled my eyes, hoping Manic could keep his dick in his pants long enough.

Shifting in my seat, I held up my phone, trying to zoom in to get some better images. But the goddamn streetlight in the back was fucking up the lighting, distorting the pictures.

"Oh, I know that sound," Manic said excitedly when the rumble of hog engines came from the distance.

"It's gotta be the Sixes." I straightened as adrenaline manifested in my veins. I was right. Slither was keeping the Sixes busy, distracting them while he had his men take care of the shipment of snow coming in.

I dialed Granite's number, keeping my eyes on Slither

and the woman in the red dress. Granite answered on the first ring. "Yeah?"

"Tell me you got something, brother."

"Oh, shit's going down right now. A truck is getting filled with snow as we speak."

I bit my lip, feeling fucking euphoric at the prospects that we might have Slither by the motherfucking balls.

"Get as many pictures as possible. And we were right. Slither is distracting Crow and his crew."

"Fucker thinks he can outsmart us."

I leaned back in the seat. "We got him, brother. We got him."

I hung up, eyes still glued on the scene in front of me. Crow got off his hog, and I was focused on Slither walking toward him when something caught my eye. The woman in red, her arm was covered in a sleeve tattoo, and something seemed oddly familiar about her.

I grabbed my phone and zoomed in on the woman— more specifically, her tattooed arm. I snapped the picture and leaned back, studying the image.

"What you got?" Manic leaned over.

"The girl," I zoomed in on the picture I took, "she seems familiar to you?"

Manic stared at the image. "Nah. But she's fit as fuck, though."

There was something about her. I couldn't place it. I looked back out the window, holding the phone to take more pictures when she flipped her hair over her shoulder... and time just fucking stopped.

"Wraith."

"What?" Manic scooted over to get a better look.

"It's Wraith."

"No way."

"Jesus." Without thinking twice, I jumped out of the van and darted across the street.

"Yo, Onyx. What the fuck, man?" Manic followed. "Get back in the fucking van. Jesus Christ."

I couldn't. I couldn't get back in the van because that woman in the red dress was my fucking woman. How the fuck did Slither get to her?

"Onyx, man. What the fuck are you doing?"

I started rushing. "I'm not about to let him hurt another one of our girls."

"Stop, okay? Let's call Granite and Dutch first before we rush over there and get our asses handed to us."

I reached behind my back, pulling out my gun. This motherfucker was going down tonight, and I didn't give a shit whether the entire Sixes crew was here. The closer I got, the clearer I saw her face. It was her, but she looked different. Her hair was different, her make-up was different. And the fact that she was wearing a mini dress and heels made no fucking sense. Where were her jeans? Her boots? Her motherfucking bad-ass expression? The sleeve tattoo on her arm was about the only thing I recognized about her.

"Onyx, stop! Jesus," I heard Manic curse behind me, "I always knew a motherfucking woman would get him killed one day."

There was a soft little voice inside my head urging me to retreat, to step back and stay in the shadows. The president of the American Street Kings knew it was foolish to go into the snake pit without backup, without a fucking plan. But the man in me, the man who marked that woman standing there, made her his, that man was ready to pull a Juggernaut on all their motherfucking asses, wrecking through them in order to get her as far away from Slither as possible.

My feet hit pavement, and I felt the adrenaline burst through my insides. "Wraith."

She turned. "Onyx?"

I aimed my gun right at Slither, who stood closely next to her. "Step away from her, man."

"Onyx, stop." She tried to step in between Slither and me, but I moved to the side, gun aimed, rage loaded, and finger ready to pull the motherfucking trigger.

"You die tonight, you sick bastard."

Slither started cackling like a maniac, and I'd never seen his expression filled with so much amusement before.

"Onyx." Wraith jumped in front of me.

I gave her a quick once-over. "Did he hurt you? Did this fucker hurt you?"

"No, he didn't hurt me."

"He's still fucking dying." I straightened my arm, finger on the trigger. It was all happening so fast, not even Crow and his crew had a chance to intervene.

"Onyx. Stop!" Wraith's voice cracked through the night, drowning out all the noise. When I looked at her, I could see her complexion had paled and the shock that shackled her blue irises. Something wasn't right, here. I could feel it in my gut. From the corner of my eye, I saw Crow cross his arms while Slither stepped closer to Wraith.

"Get away from her, motherfucker!" I wanted to tear his goddamn skin off for thinking he had the right to stand so close to her.

"Onyx, stop." She took a step my way, but Slither grabbed her arm. And that was when the beast in me took full control, grabbing the motherfucking wheel and riding straight into the flames of hell.

"Take your goddamn hands off her, Slither. I don't need another reason to fucking kill you." As I moved forward, already seeing his face painted with his own damn blood while my bullet cracked through his skull, Crow stepped in front of me, blocking my view, making it impossible for me to get a shot.

"Put away the gun, Onyx," he said softly.

I glared at him. "This ain't your fight, Crow. Step out of my way."

"This might not be my fight, but this is my goddamn club, and you are not soiling my street with this filthy fucker's blood. You feel me?"

Manic finally caught up to me. "Onyx." He leaned closer but didn't say anything further. He knew better than to tell me what to fucking do in front of all these people.

"Get out of my way, Crow," I snarled, a monster determined to dare the devil.

Crow merely took a step closer. "Think about this, VP."

"President," I shot back. "I'm the president now."

His eyes widened. "What? Something happen to Granite?"

"No." I looked over his shoulder at Slither, hiding like a coward behind the sea of Sixes. "My brother stepped down."

A look of enlightenment crossed Crow's face. "Because of the deal he made with Slither."

"Yeah."

Crow turned and glanced half-way at Slither and Wraith before turning back to me. "So, the deal is no longer valid."

"Nope."

"What the fuck you talking about?" Slither stepped up, guiding Wraith behind him. It was like my vision zeroed in on that one spot on her elbow where he touched her, and it turned everything around me to different shades of red.

"Take your hands off her, Slither. This is your last motherfucking warning."

Crow glanced from me to Slither, and back to me, and it was clear as fucking daylight the man was amused as fuck. "Hold on. So, you're the president of the Kings now?"

I nodded. "That's right. Fucker over there didn't think we'd find a way around our little deal. Well, I'd say we pretty much fucked him in the ass."

Crow smirked. "I did not see that one coming."

"Yeah," I glowered at Slither, "neither did he."

Slither's face fell, and I didn't think I had ever seen him without a smug grin. Like me, he knew he was fucked. The deal between him and Granite was no longer valid, which meant the Sixes' business was fair game. But right now, none of that shit mattered. The only thing that mattered was getting Wraith out of here before he ended up hurting her as well.

"Wraith, come on." I gestured toward me, but she didn't move. "Wraith, get the fuck away from him."

But she didn't move. She only stood there, staring at me like her life was about to end.

"Oh, this is good," Slither commented from the side. "This is really, really good." The smug grin that had disappeared for a second was back, and he reached out, placing his hand around her waist, pulling her in next to him.

I snarled, baring fucking teeth like an animal. I tried to launch forward when Crow stepped in front of me, holding me back. "Not the time, man."

"Let go of her, Slither," I ordered over Crow's shoulder, his hands still firmly pressed against my chest. There was no way in hell I'd let this monster hurt anyone else I cared about.

Slither tightened his grip around her waist, and she gasped, her face pale, eyes frozen. "Where's my manners?" Slither started. "I should introduce you two."

"Slither, don't." Wraith turned away from me so to face him. "Don't do this."

But he ignored her, keeping his glare pinned on me. "Dahlia, meet Onyx, apparently the new president of the Kings."

"Slither—"

"Onyx," he smirked, "meet Dahlia. My sister."

Religion wasn't my thing. Gods, angels, devils, and demons—I didn't want to believe there were higher powers playing a game of chess with us as their pawns. But at that very second, I was sure the gods had pulled the universe right out from under me.

My heart was lodged in my throat, my skin clammy and cold even though it felt like the heat of Satan scorched my inside. "What?"

Slither grinned. "You heard me."

"Oh, fuck." Manic stilled next to me.

"What the fuck is he talking about?" I looked at Wraith.

Her silence, the way she just stood there staring back at me, I could have sworn I heard her scream the answer I didn't want to hear. That Slither was telling the truth. It wasn't a sick, twisted ploy to mindfuck me. It was the truth. It was right there on her face, her pale cheeks, and red lips.

I cleared my throat, trying to stop my heart from choking me so I could take a damn breath.

"You're—" I choked on the words, swallowing hard. "You're his sister?"

"Of course she is." Slither pulled her closer, rubbing his cheek against hers. "Can't you see the resemblance?"

I knew he was being a melodramatic fuck, milking this grave moment for all it was worth. But there actually was a resemblance, something I never would have noticed did he not push his goddamn face against hers.

"Wraith, is he your fucking brother?" I gritted, heart about to rip from my chest.

Without looking at me, she merely nodded, no trace of the confidence she always seemed to carry.

"No," I breathed in disbelief as I stepped back. "No, no, no. This isn't true."

"Oh, yes, yes, yes," Slither mocked.

While my heart turned into shards of glass tearing through my spine, it was impossible for me to form any kind of coherent thought. A sentence. A motherfucking word. My entire world just got shot to shit, and I didn't know how the fuck I remained standing.

Crow turned to face Slither, and by the way Slither straightened, letting go of Wraith, I could only guess Crow was glaring at him. "So, let me get this straight. She's your sister?"

Slither lifted an arm. "Am I speaking fucking Japanese? Yes, she's my sister."

I kept my attention on Wraith, her eyes red and cheeks wet. She was crying, but I was too busy clawing the knife out of my back to care.

Crow walked closer, arms hanging down his sides. "Earlier, you said she was one of your girls," he stilled, "but that she was mine for tonight."

"Jesus Christ," I muttered, pulling at the roots of my hair, my skull practically in fucking flames.

"Yeah," Slither responded without hesitating.

Crow glanced toward me with a frown, then back to the Slither. "So, you're telling me your sister is your clubwhore?"

"I'm not a clubwhore," Wraith spat out.

"Shut your goddamn mouth." Slither glared her way, and I was ready to smash his skull against the sidewalk.

He walked up to Crow, clearly picking up on a vibe from him. "How we do things is none of anyone's business."

Crow held up his hand, his entire demeanor turning hostile—even I could see it simply by looking at his back. "You brought your little sister here, to my club, with the intention of whoring her?"

"Motherfucker," I cursed under my breath.

Slither reached for Wraith's hand, but she pulled away. I didn't know why that eased me a little, but it did.

"This is business, Crow," Slither stated.

"True. But she's your sister, man. She's fucking blood. And that's one line we don't cross here. We don't fuck with blood."

"That part, you got right. My blood. She's *my* blood. And I'll do with her what I want to."

Confused and angry, I looked her way, my heart slowly bleeding out. "Is he making you do this? Is he forcing you to do this?"

Wraith didn't move. She didn't confirm or deny, and it was unsettling, to say the least.

"Wraith!" My voice sliced through the dark, and she yelped. "Answer me, goddammit. Is he fucking making you do this?"

She bit her lip, eyes downcast and shoulders slumped. "No," she whispered.

"Excuse me?"

"No." Her gaze cut to mine. "He's not forcing me to do anything."

My knees were no longer strong enough to keep me upright, so I crouched, hand in my hair. "Jesus Christ. This is not happening." I straightened. "This is not fucking happening!" I yelled, and I wanted to break and kill something. I wanted to feel bone crack in my palms, see blood flow over my hands and stick to my nails.

"Oh, poor lover boy," Slither mocked. "I hope you at least got a good fuck out of this, since the only reason she even looked your way was because I told her to."

And here I thought the knife couldn't twist any deeper into my back. "Wraith, tell me this isn't what I think this is." I gritted my teeth.

Again, she only stood there, pale as a ghost.

I frowned with disbelief. "So, I was just a target? You used me, to what? Get some inside information for your brother, here?"

"Ding, ding, ding." Slither laughed. "Seems like you're not as stupid as I thought you were."

"I'm sorry," Wraith muttered, tears lapping against her lips.

"Oh, God," I breathed. "Today at the beach, when you talked about your past, and your brother, you were talking about...him?"

Tears kept streaming down her face, red blotches covering her face.

I grimaced. "Was any of it actually true, or was it all just a bunch of bullshit you fed me?"

"No. I told you the truth today." Her bottom lip trembled, her jaw ticking as she tried to suppress the tears—tears that meant nothing to me. Tears that were unable to crack through the concrete wall of betrayal.

I retreated, the sight of her making my stomach twist inside out. "You're a fucking liar. A fake." That goddamn knife in my back jabbed all the way through my motherfucking heart.

Slither rolled his eyes. "Cut the drama, would you? You're gonna give me an aneurysm."

"Yo, shut the fuck up," Manic said from behind me, and my instincts instantly flared up like the motherfucking Fourth of July. Slither reached for his gun, and so did the rest of his crew.

I had mine aimed and ready by my next breath, but Crow's voice erupted through the chaos. "The first person who pulls a motherfucking trigger here on my street will choke on his own fucking blood, I swear to Christ!" His glare moved from me to Slither as he pointed at his crew standing behind him. "Both of you are heavily outnumbered here, so don't fuck with me on my turf, or neither of you will see daylight again."

Slither's top lip lifted with a snarl, and I could see the bloodlust in his eyes. He wanted me dead almost as much as I wanted to bury him. But right now, the stench of betrayal was far stronger than the hunt for blood.

Bold, brave, and hurt like hell, I walked up to her, not giving two flying fucks that Slither was standing right next to her with a loaded gun in his hand. All I cared about was hearing the truth from her lips. "So, all this time, you were being the Python clubwhore who spread her legs to impress big brother, here." Her expression was pained, like I had just slapper her in the face, but I didn't give a fuck, my insides slowly being torn to shreds.

I stepped closer, so close I could smell her perfume. Perfume she didn't wear for me. Not tonight.

She looked at me, black mascara smudges sticking to the skin around her eyes. If deceit and lies didn't cling to my soul like dirt, I might have mistaken her despondent look for regret. Remorse. Maybe even a broken heart.

I bit my lip, and I no longer saw the beautiful woman who tempted me with her full lips, sharp tongue, and curvy body. I no longer saw the woman I would move heaven and hell for, give her my world just to keep her in my bed, keep her close to me. She was no longer the woman whose touch thrilled me, whose kisses seduced me.

All I saw was the Python clubwhore who accomplished what she had set out to do. Ruin me.

"Onyx—" She reached out for me, but I pulled back, letting out low snarl.

"Don't," I warned.

"I didn't mean—"

Slither pulled her back. "I'm going to take all this melodramatic bullshit as our cue to leave."

Her eyes pleaded with me, like she was begging me to ask her to stay. But I'd rather swallow glass. The anger simmering in my veins was too much. The scent of betrayal was too fucking pungent in the air around us.

"Slither," Crow called the same time two of his men flanked the snake and his sister. God, I threw up in my mouth a little, thinking of her being his sister.

"I don't do business with men who have no respect for family," Crow growled. "Don't come back here."

"Excuse me?" Slither narrowed his eyes. "Since when do you take the moral high ground?"

"Get the fuck off my turf, and I better not see your face around here."

Judging by the animosity that pulsed all around us, it seemed like we didn't need proof of the Pythons' hands in the Sixes' drug trade after all. All it took was for Crow to see for himself what a low-life piece of shit Slither really was.

Slither wiped his mouth with the back of his hand, pure hatred beaming from his eyes. "This isn't over. I can promise you that."

While Crow and Slither had the stare-off of the motherfucking century, all I could do was look at her. Stare at her, wondering how it was possible for a lie to have felt so fucking right ever since it all started.

Another tear trickled down her cheek. "This isn't how I intended for things to turn out."

I watched with a wildly beating heart as she looked from me to her brother, then back to me. It was there, every conflicting emotion she felt was right there in the blue shades of her eyes.

"Dahlia!" Slither scolded. "Shut the fuck up, and let's go."

"Then what the fuck did you intend to happen, huh?" I bit my lip, hand shaking while I still clutched the gun. "You pretended to be someone you're not, doing his bidding. And even after you saw what he did to Neon, after you witnessed the hell she's going through, you still came back to him. Still stand next to him?" Disbelief crashed with fury, and I didn't know whether it was my heart or my goddamn mind that was breaking. I leaned forward, shooting a glare right at her pretty fucking face. "You're not just a clubwhore. You're a monster. Just. Like. Him."

The look in her eyes scared me. It told tales of loyalty, history, and family secrets. Secrets she would keep...in order to protect her brother.

She whimpered, placing her palm in front of her mouth. "I didn't mean to hurt you, Onyx. I'm sorry. This wasn't supposed—"

"Fuck this bullshit." I turned my back on her and on everyone else who stood there watching the show. I couldn't stand staring at her for a second longer.

"Onyx!" I heard her call after me, but I ignored her. I ignored the piece of my heart urging me to turn around and go to her. I ignored everything inside me that wanted me to go back and beg her to tell me all this was nothing but some sick, twisted, fucked-up joke. She had made a fool of me. Played me. Lied to me like I was nothing but a street rat, and not even the plea in her voice as she called my name could make me see past that.

"Onyx! Please!"

I couldn't stop myself from walking away.

19

ONYX

Watching her get into a car, driving away with Slither tailing her, I wanted to claw my own heart out. My mind was struggling to make sense of it all, how she deceived me since day one. The connection I thought we shared, the undeniable attraction was all a lie. Everything was a lie. Every touch, every kiss, every heated breath wasn't real.

After today, at the beach, I was sure we connected on some deeper level with her sharing a piece of her past with me. I was convinced it was a step in the right direction to have her trust me with her secrets. But now, every goddamn word she spoke to me today felt like knives of lies cutting through my chest.

"You okay, man?" Manic slammed the cage door, and I stared after the car that eventually disappeared into the distance.

"Yeah, I'm good." Liar.

"This is some fucked up bullshit."

I roughed my hand through my hair, trying to swallow this heaviness lodged in my throat.

"I can't believe she's his sister."

I bit the inside of my mouth, thinking of the blood that coursed through her veins being the same as that of my enemy.

"Crazy shit," Manic muttered, and I lost it.

Slamming my first against the steering wheel, I cursed as the rage poisoned me. All this time, I was sure I had no more space left in me to be consumed by hate. But I was wrong. Apparently, there seemed to have been another little empty corner in my soul which was now occupied with something worse than hate, or fury.

Heartache.

Manic finally shut up, not daring to say another word as I kicked at the motherfucking dash. "Jesus fucking Christ!" I screamed, my heart pounding against my ribs like a sledge-hammer, cracking bone.

Harley engines roared, coming from a distance.

"Granite and Dutch." Manic stated the obvious.

I got out of the van and lit a cigarette, pacing across the asphalt as they parked their hogs on the side of the road.

"What happened?" Granite walked right up to me, probably sensing that things were all fucked up inside my head.

"Wraith." I couldn't even say her name without wanting to break something.

"What about her?" Granite looked from me to Manic, but Manic knew better than to speak for me.

I took a long drag from my cigarette before facing him. "She's his sister."

"Whose sister?"

Another drag. "Slither." I breathed his name out with a cloud of smoke. "She's Slither's sister."

"What?" Granite's eyebrows curved with confusion. "He has a sister?"

"Yup."

"Hold up," Dutch joined in. "Wraith is Slither's sister? How, when, and what the fuck?"

I flicked the cigarette on the side of the road. "She was a rat."

"Jesus," Granite breathed, pulling his hand through his hair, staring down at the ground. "What happened here?"

I hunched down, clenching my fists. "She came with Slither tonight, meeting the Sixes."

"Why?"

I glanced up at him. "She's the Pythons' clubwhore. Well, sorta."

"What are you talking about?"

I swallowed, the words too sharp to utter, afraid it would slice my insides into pieces. I indicated toward Manic, urging him to tell the story further.

He cleared his throat. "Slither brought her here tonight as part of the distraction."

I cursed a string of f-bombs, the thought of another man touching her tearing me the fuck apart.

Unable to contain the rage, I jumped up and slammed my fist into the panel of the van, causing a huge dent... almost like the hole in my chest.

"Onyx." I turned when I heard Crow's voice. "I have to give it to you. Some stunt you pulled, finding a way out of the deal with Slither." He looked at Granite. "You have my respect, man, putting your club's needs before your own."

Granite shrugged. "I'd do everything for my men."

Crow glanced at me, eyes narrowed. "We down for business?"

"Yeah, man." I probably should have been a little more excited over the fact that we just got our biggest client and ally back, but everything about this night felt off. Distorted. Fucked the hell up.

"Crow," Granite started, "we got something you should know."

"What?"

Granite shot me a knowing look, slightly nodding for me to chip in to the conversation.

I cleared my throat. "You probably heard about the new snow on the street."

"Yeah, I heard. I've been tapping into every resource I have, but we can't find the fuckers."

"It's the Pythons."

Crow stiffened, dark eyes narrowed into angry slits. "Slither?"

I rubbed the back of my neck. "Yeah. This whole setup tonight was a ploy to keep you occupied while their next shipment hit town."

Granite stepped up, holding out his phone so Crow could see the pictures they took. "It's been the Pythons all along."

Crow's expression went from pale, to red, to downright fucking dark. "So, while this fucker has been taking my money, he's been fucking with my business too?"

I shrugged. "Seems like it."

Crow whistled, waving a few of his guys to join the conversation. He turned halfway, whispering something to his VP before facing us again. "Before the crack of dawn, Slither and his crew will take their last breath. You in?"

"Fuck, yes." There was no need to check with my crew, no need to take a vote. I already knew where everyone's minds were. This had been coming for years, the day when we finally took back what was rightfully ours, giving that son of bitch what he deserved. And after his latest stunt, using his sister as a rat, infiltrating us by fooling me—now I wanted his blood more than ever.

Crow nodded. "We ride now. Make sure you're packing heavy shit." He turned and walked off to the rest of his crew.

Granite stepped up to me. "You okay with this?"

"That's shitty question, brother. Of course I'm okay with this. We've been waiting years for this."

"Yeah, but this whole thing with Wraith complicates—"

"It ain't complicating shit. She's with our enemy, that makes her an enemy too." Not wanting to spend another second on the topic, I faced Manic. "Call Ink. Tell him this shit is going down tonight. He's finally getting the blood he wants."

"Onyx—" Granite followed me to the van, but I held up my hand, my back turned to him.

"Don't. I'm good. I just want all of this to end." I hopped into the cage and slammed the door shut. "And tonight, it ends."

"She'll be there."

"She made her choice."

"Listen," he placed his arm on the edge of the open window, "one thing I've learned, when it comes to Slither, nothing is as it seems."

I glared his way. "What are you saying?"

"What I'm saying is I know you're hurt. I know what it feels like to realize you have a weakness after thinking there was nothing that could limit you. Nothing that can break you."

"What's your point?" Last thing I needed was some psychobabble bullshit from my brother who suddenly thought he became an expert in life simply because he found an old lady to keep his bed warm at night.

"My point is don't make harsh decisions without getting all the facts...especially when you're hurt."

"I'm fine."

"Just like Ink's fine?"

I pulled my eyes into slits. "Don't compare me to Ink."

"You're both fueled by your emotions. Ink's rage...and you, your pride."

I clenched my jaw, and I had to fill my head with visions of Slither's dead body rather than Wraith's face, her tears. All it did was make me feel shit I didn't want to feel.

"Are we sure there's not a bigger picture here?"

"What are you talking about?"

"I dunno, man. I just think when it comes to Slither, there's always a motherfucking bigger picture."

Clutching the steering wheel, knuckles turning white, I thought back to our confrontation. Slither's cocky attitude. Her tears. Crow's surprise. And the goddamn knife in my back.

The image of that son of bitch standing next to her, having his hand on her—an act of possession—made me sick. How he looked at me with that smirk on his face, knowing exactly how fucked up it all was. At least there was one part of that entire conversation that went our way...the motherfucking look on his face when he realized we trumped his ass, that Granite was no longer president. The look of shock on his ugly face was priceless, the moment nothing short of triumphant glee. He never saw it coming.

He never saw it coming.

"Wait." My thoughts scattered.

"What is it?"

"He didn't know."

Granite frowned. "Didn't know what?"

"But she did."

"Onyx, you're not making sense. What the fuck are you on about?"

"Wraith." I looked at him. "She knew I was president. She knew you stepped down, and that I took your place."

"How?

"I told her."

"Okay." He seemed confused.

I shifted in my seat, adrenaline swooshing through me. "Wraith knew, but Slither didn't. That means she didn't tell him."

Granite tapped on the edge of the window. "It's some big shit info for her to keep to herself if she was a rat."

"Yeah. What the fuck does this mean, though?"

He shrugged. "Like I said, when it comes to Slither, there's always a bigger picture."

I put the van in gear. "I'm about to find out what that bigger fucking picture is."

Manic got into the van. "Ink's on his way."

Granite stepped back, and I revved the engine. "This is it, brother, the day we've been waiting years for."

FOR THE LAST FIFTEEN YEARS, I didn't think I had a heart. I lived my life like I had nothing to lose. Like I felt nothing. A void. A wraith. But now, my tears painted a different picture, created an image of someone who felt something. Who had a heart. Seeing the look on Onyx's face made me die a slow death inside. I wasn't even aware there was something that resembled a heartbeat in this black soul of mine, not until it cracked wide open when I watched Onyx realize I had betrayed him. Played him. Lied to him.

It was summer, yet I was clutching my arms tightly against my chest as if to ward off the cold. I was relieved when Slither didn't get in the car with me, one of his prospects driving me home. I couldn't face him, not when I felt so broken. He'd see it as a weakness, scold me for not turning off my feelings, my humanity. It was something I had mastered years ago, yet all it took was a few encounters and a passionate love affair with Onyx to make me forget I had the means to switch off my ability to feel. Now I cursed him for it. If he didn't make me feel again, I wouldn't have been sitting in the back seat of a car crying like I got my heart broken.

All these years, Slither was the one man I trusted. He was the one man I knew would protect me, keep the bad people away. But after tonight, I wasn't so sure anymore. What if he *was* one of the bad people?

I pulled off my shoes as I got out of the car, refusing to torture myself further with stiletto heels, and ran barefoot into the building I'd called home for so long and straight to my room. My bedroom wasn't much, but at least it was mine. Slither had the room soundproofed so I didn't have to listen to their wild parties, fights, screaming, and chaos whenever it erupted. This was like my own little corner in the world where I was free of everything and everyone.

With a bed in the corner, lilac sheets draped over it, a bedside table with a matching chest of drawers, it was your typical female bedroom. But it was the only little space in the world I could call my own. Where I didn't have to wear a mask or pretend to be this whole other person, when in fact, I was nothing but a broken porcelain doll. No matter how many times you tried to glue the pieces back together, the cracks would always remain. And all those times I had been with Onyx, he made me think the cracks were gone—that I had somehow gone from broken to undented. Especially when he touched me, something I never got pleasure from before him—a man's touch. In the past, I had endured it, never relished it. Until him.

Tossing my shoes on the floor, I dragged my tired body over to the bed while unzipping the side of my dress, still seeing flashes of Onyx's face in my head. Never in a million years did I think I'd regret hurting someone the way I hurt him.

Exhaling and closing my eyes, I stood there in the

middle of the room thinking of birthday candles. If I had one more shot at making a wish, it would be to go back to the night I thrust myself into Onyx's life for the first time. If I could have done it over, I would have walked right past his table and not glanced back once, then just end up telling Slither Onyx wasn't interested. Shot me down on the very first try. Then I wouldn't have been trapped in this shitstorm right now, and I wouldn't have Onyx's face haunting me.

"Care to tell me what the fuck happened tonight?"

"Jesus Christ, Slither." I gulped. "Stop doing that. Don't you fucking knock?"

He shrugged. "Not when it's my house." The door clicked closed behind him, and it instantly felt like all the oxygen was sucked out of the room, the space getting smaller and smaller with each passing second. "Did you know?"

"Did I know what?"

"That Onyx is president of the Kings."

I swallowed hard, shifting from one leg to the other. There was no use in trying to lie. No one knew me as well as my brother did. He had the ability to see right through me, spot a lie even before I opened my mouth.

"Yes," I breathed. "I knew."

It happened so fast, I didn't have time to react or to even think. The next thing I knew, Slither had his hand around my throat, slamming my back against the wall.

I grabbed at his wrist, trying to pull his hand away, but he was too strong, his grip only tightening, making it hard to breathe.

"You knew? You fucking knew and didn't tell me?"

"You're hurting me."

His face came within inches of mine, his angry breaths

burning my skin. "Because of you, I stood there looking like a fucking idiot." He jerked my face toward him. "Because you didn't tell me, those motherfuckers caught me off guard, and I looked weak. Stupid."

"Glenn—"

I swallowed my words when the back of his hand collided with my cheek, the sting of his rage striking me in the face. He let go of my throat, and I tumbled to the floor, my aching knees nothing compared to the fire on my cheek. Tears burned as I pressed my palm against the searing flesh.

"What else do you know? What else did you keep from me?" He stalked closer, and I tried to crawl back, tried to get away from him. "What else?" he bellowed, spit flying from his seething mouth.

"Nothing. I know nothing else."

"Liar!"

He grabbed my ankles, his grip tight and merciless. I tried fighting, kicking, begging him to let me go, but he dragged me across the floor, and with a hard jerk, he slid me headfirst into the wall, stars exploding around me.

Clutching my head, trying to think through the pain, he crouched, grabbing my throat and pulling me halfway off the floor. When I opened my eyes, staring into his, I gasped. Everything was dark, so dark. It was like the darkest pits of hell had consumed him, the scales on his skin coming to life and moving like a serpent about to strike. The last time I saw him like this was when...was the night he killed them.

"After everything I did for you, this is how you repay me?"

I sobbed, fear burning holes in my stomach. "Please—"

"I killed them for you. I became a murderer for you, and this is what you do to me?" His words were poison, lethal and fierce, aimed straight at my heart. "Maybe all the luxuries I've given you, this good life you've been living because of me, made you forget where you actually came from."

"Good life?" I narrowed my eyes, and through the tears, I finally found my voice. "What good life? Like they all said tonight, I'm nothing but a clubwhore for you."

"If you were a clubwhore I'd have my men fuck you in every motherfucking hole. But maybe that's what you deserve since you betrayed me," he snarled before striking another hand across my face. This time I tasted blood...my blood. The metallic taste brought back so many bad memories—memories of fists, faces, dirty words, and pain. So much pain.

I tried to turn on my front, tried to claw my way across the floor, when he reached for my hair, pulling me to my feet. "Glenn, stop! Please."

"And then you even shared our secrets with him."

"No."

"You told him about our past. Jesus, you're just an ungrateful whore."

I reached back, nails clawing at the flesh of his arms, trying to get him to let go. But my fight only seemed to anger him more—adding more fuel to the already raging fire in him.

Pain burst through the side of my face when he slammed me into the wall again, this time pinning me in place with his body. There was no time for me to figure out what the hell was happening; all I knew was this wasn't my brother. This was the man who murdered those who hurt us.

"Do you remember that night, sis?"

I closed my eyes, willing the memories away.

"Do you remember the flames? The smell of rotten, burning flesh?"

"Please—"

"I remember it. I remember it like it was yesterday." He tightened his grip in my hair, pushing me harder against the wall. "I remember their screams, their blood. The way they begged me to stop, to not kill them."

"Oh, God." Bile started to move up my throat.

"But I showed them no mercy, just like they showed us none when we begged. When we pleaded for them to stop because Mom needed her fucking fix. And God knew, Mom couldn't go without the fucking shit she pumped in her arm. But you know what I remember the most of that night?" He leaned closer. "You." I felt the two parts of his tongue slither against my ear. "I remember the fifteen-year-old girl who stood in her doorway and watched while I hacked away at our mother, and our father, and the men they brought home that night."

God, I remembered it too. I remembered the smell of the blood, the smell of death.

"You merely stood there, not saying a word, not moving. Doing nothing. To stop. Me. You liked it, didn't you? You liked watching me and my friends butcher them. Say it."

I whimpered, seeing their faces. Mom and Dad. Faces beaten. Arms and legs broken. Blood everywhere. Glenn's friends killed the men Mom and Dad brought home that night, and they helped him butcher Dad. But Mom? He killed her himself, refused to let anyone else touch her. While I stood in the bedroom door watching as he tied her up, she cried out to me, held out her hand, pleading for me to help her. To save her—just like I had cried so many times for her to not let those dirty men take me. But I just stood there, watching as Glenn tore all her clothes off, ripping them to threads, humiliating her by letting her lie on the ground naked, tied up, and stuffing her dirty panties into her mouth to keep her from screaming.

I can still remember a part of me thinking it was wrong, that what they were doing was wrong. But another part of me, the biggest part, convinced me it was justice. It was payback, Mom's atonement for what she had done to us— all because she needed her fucking drugs. After watching them torture her for an hour, slapping her, kicking her, pissing on her, I walked over, crouched beside her and gently tucked her hair behind her ear. And I can still remember the words I said to her that night, the soft words I whispered in her ear. *"You're a big girl now."* And then I walked out, closing the door behind me, leaving her alone with Glenn and his friends. With every step I took down that hall, every shackle my parents had locked around my soul broke into pieces. Every blood smear that was splattered on the wall and floors was like bricks laid on my path to freedom—a path where the demons could no longer hurt me. And I smiled. I smiled like my entire world got righted, and I owed it all to my brother.

I owed him everything...which was why I would have done anything for him. Even become his clubwhore.

Tears burned my flesh, the memories cracking through every bone in my body. "Glenn, please stop this."

"Say it, sis. Say you loved watching me kill them."

"Please—"

"Say it!"

"Yes! God, yes!" I cried. "I liked watching you kill them. I didn't want you to stop." Sobs erupted, hard and aching, pouring out of me all the way from my gut.

"There she is." I felt him flex against me, and then the fear of hell ripped through my spine. "There's my girl."

"Glenn—"

"Let me tell you a little secret, Dahlia." His fingers teased along the side of my face, his chest flush against my back. "Mom's friends weren't the only ones who visited me at night. She did too."

I stilled, unable to fight after his words shook me to the core.

"That's right. Mom visited me too. Told me I was her big boy right before she made me watch porn so I could get hard. Hard for her."

My body trembled, and I closed my eyes, trying to keep the tears under control. "You never told me."

He yanked at my hair. "Of course I didn't tell you. Being raped by strange men was bad enough, but having your own mom forcing you to fuck her while she threatened to cut it off and feed it to the fucking dog, that's not something you go around sharing with people."

I pinched my eyes closed, my heart breaking for my brother all over again. Breaking for us. The pain we went through, the humiliation—God, it was so much worse for him. I realized that now.

"Glenn, I'm sorry she did that to you."

He let out a maniacal laugh. "Don't worry, sis. I got my revenge. See," he jerked me around abruptly, pinning my back against the wall, "after you closed that door, I got my revenge." He tilted his head, black eyes focused on me, his mouth pulled in an evil smirk. "Ask me how."

I swallowed hard.

"Ask me how!" he yelled.

"How?"

He smiled, a gentle finger tracing down the side of my face, his eyes following the movement. "By giving her what she wanted. By fucking her, over, and over, and over again. We took turns, my friends and I." He took my chin between his fingers, digging into my jaw. "And not just with our dicks."

I couldn't stop it. The picture he painted, the words he spewed out of his mouth, was so toxic, I couldn't keep the bile down anymore. I gagged, and he grabbed my hair, forcing me to bend over while I threw up.

"Funny, I remember her gagging a few times that day as well."

"Why are you doing this?"

He jerked me upright, craning my head back while my scalp burned as he pulled my hair. "Because tonight you showed me exactly how fucking thankful you really are."

Dragging me across the room and over to the bed, he tossed me onto the mattress like a ragdoll. Like I weighed nothing. It felt like my heart was about to claw out of my chest, my stomach stripped and torn, about to bleed out of my body.

I tried to get away, my fingers twisting into the sheets, but he held me down, my stomach on the mattress, his body flush against my back. "Glenn, please. What are you doing?" I twisted, and flexed, and tried to get out from under him, but he was too strong, his hands gripping my wrists and pinning them next to my face.

"Ever since your tenth birthday, I was forced to listen to them rape you, forced to listen to your screams and your cries."

Tears ripped from my soul, escaping down my cheeks. The fear, the panic, the uncertainty was something I hadn't felt for a very long time. But it was back...and this time it was even stronger than before.

He eased his face closer to mine. "Every damn time I heard what they did to you through the walls of our bedrooms, I felt my hate grow stronger, bolder, harder. They were hurting my little sister, and I couldn't do anything about it." His voice cracked, pain dripping from his words. "Until..." He took a breath. "Until one night those cries turned into something different. See, I was sure it would stop eventually, that you'd give up crying since they were never going to stop. So, surely, you would stop fighting, stop crying. But you didn't." He moved, flexing his hips, and horror grabbed me by the throat, choking every ounce of air from my lungs.

He was hard. He was so hard, and I could feel it press against my back. I tried to jerk free, gritting my teeth, but it was no use. I was no match for him. He just gripped me tighter, pushed harder against me. "One night while I laid on my bed listening to them rape you, listening to you crying," his lips brushed my ear, "I touched myself."

"Jesus," I sobbed, and I tried to fight by thrashing and kicking, screaming like I had the devil's touch on my back.

"That's right, little sister," he continued, cool and calm, like there was nothing fucked up about it. "I jerked off while you got raped. And after that, whenever Mommy came to visit me in my room, I didn't need to watch porn to get hard." His split tongue slithered along my ear, down the skin in my neck, and I shuddered, my entire body trembling. "All I had to do was think about you and your screams that became like a fucking melody to me. That's all I needed to get hard for mommy dearest."

He thrust against me, and I bit into my tongue, the taste of blood blasting through my mouth—the taste of repulsion and terror.

"You feel that? I just have to talk about it, and my cock gets hard for you."

"You're sick!"

He laughed. "Tell me something I don't know."

"You have to stop this, Glenn. You need help."

"No. What I needed was my little sister to be on my side, to be loyal to me. But you betrayed me."

"I didn't."

"You did!"

"How? How did I betray you?" I continued to thrash, but it seemed like my fight only made him stronger.

"By not telling me the Kings were about to fool me by letting Onyx become president. A little fucking loophole they found with our deal. You didn't tell me!" he yelled, and stars exploded behind my eyes when his fist collided against my skull, my teeth clattering together. The blow resonated in my head, my tongue bleeding and temples aching. I stopped moving, a numbness flooding over my body. There was no more strength in me, my limbs paralyzed and my mind dizzy.

Flashes. Images. Pain. I couldn't focus. Everything was a blur. Except *him*. *His* face.

Onyx.

Through the haze, I heard him speak—my brother. The man who was supposed to protect me. Who promised me he would always keep me safe. Then why did his breath feel repugnant against my neck? Why did his words slice through me like broken glass, cutting my insides to pieces? Why did his touch feel vile, corrupted, sordid? Wrong.

"Onyx was right." His words became clearer. "You are a clubwhore. And what kind of president would I be if I didn't give my clubwhore the attention she deserved?"

When I felt his hand between my legs, tears followed, like lava flowing down, erupting from the flames that burned me to ash.

"Please." My voice was barely a whisper, my head on the verge of exploding. "Don't do this."

"I've wanted to do this for so long, little sis. Ever since I realized you look just like...her."

"No." I sobbed, and my arms tingled, my feet prickling as my strength slowly returned. Everything inside me begged my body to fight, and I jerked my arms, trying to loosen his grip. I didn't open my eyes. I didn't dare. There was no way I'd be able to look into my brother's eyes and survive it, not while he was doing this to me.

"Fight me, Dahlia. Fight me, scream for me the way you screamed for them."

"Don't—"

I jerked my head from side to side, my body flailing and thrashing. Somehow, I managed to free one arm, and I tried clawing at his face from over my shoulder, hitting, scratching, tearing at anything I could get my hands on. But he was so much stronger than I was, like he knew my every move.

Of course he did. He'd been a victim himself. He knew how one's instincts reacted, what it made you do.

Pushing him off me, I tried to struggle up the bed, but he grabbed my ankles, twisting me around with a violent jerk. No matter how hard I tried to keep him from forcing me on my stomach, he was just too strong.

I kicked and screamed, but it was no use. The second he had me on my stomach, I tried to reach for the headboard of the bed, but he pulled me down, and then I heard it. The tear of fabric as he ripped my dress down the back.

"See, Dahlia. I'm not as bad as you think I am." He climbed on top of me, his knee pressing hard into my back, forcing me to stay in place as he twisted my arms behind me. "I told myself I would never hurt you, not unless you gave me a very good reason to."

I continued to fight as he tied my wrists. Whatever he used pinched my skin around my arms, and then he straddled me. That was the moment I realized there was no way I'd be able to fight him anymore. Not while he had me pinned in place with his body and tied up.

"Glenn, you don't know what you're doing."

"I'm teaching my little sister a lesson." He leaned down, his chest flush against my naked back, gently brushing my hair from the side of my neck. "A lesson I've been dying to teach you for so long."

"Is that what you did to Neon?"

He stilled.

"I know what you did to her. I saw her."

"She was merely collateral damage."

"You fucked her up, Glenn. You raped her, and now you want to rape me too." I stopped thrashing, taking a deep breath as I tried to calm my wildly beating heart. "You turned into one of them. You're no better than the men who hurt us, than Mom and Dad, who never protected us." With every word, my fear turned into fury. "I was a fool to ever think you loved me."

"But I do." His lips brushed against my ear. "I do love you. Don't you see that? I've always loved you, but you hurt me. You betrayed me."

"No, you're betraying me. Remember that day you came to my room after my tenth birthday? You promised me that the day you were big enough, you would make it all right. You won't let anyone else hurt me. But now you're hurting me."

His tongue traced along my ear. "You deserve it."

"Then do it. Hurt me. Rape me. Kill me." All my strength drained out of me as I surrendered to the darkness, my body sagging into the mattress. "I'm done fighting. There's no need to fight when you're already a rotting corpse."

A heavy silence fell around us, and I allowed myself to

take a breath. But as the air settled in my lungs, I felt his hand slowly travel down my side, fingers wrapping around my knee before jerking it up, spreading my legs wide. The warm summer air felt like ice against my nakedness, and I wanted to die right there. If there was a way for me to end my life in that moment, I would have done it without hesitating.

I bit my lips, the saltiness of my pain coating my tongue. After years of being free from that hell, I found myself thrown back there again—by another person I trusted. Another person who had sworn to protect me, yet now he was the one about to hurt me.

Forcing one of his thighs beneath my leg, keeping me in place, I knew this wasn't the first time he did this. He moved like a fucking expert, anticipating my every move, knowing exactly how I would fight back. My brother had done this before. The man I trusted with my life had destroyed others the same way we were ruined.

"Don't worry, little sis," I heard the sound of his zipper, and my blood ran cold, "I'll do better than all those men. I'll make you enjoy it."

"God, please. Glenn, stop," I sobbed, trying one last time to struggle against his hold, but it was no use. I was that ten-year-old girl again, unable to fight, no match against the demons hellbent on taking me. Ruining me. Destroying me. Leaving nothing but dead butterflies in their wake.

Strong thighs kept me in place, a hand keeping my arms from moving when his fingers traveled up the inside of my thigh, like devil claws infecting my skin.

When I felt him drag his hard dick down the slit of my ass, I gagged, choking on my own cries. I was sure my tears had turned into blood, the way it ached in my chest, my stomach twisted in barbed wire while my body burned.

Trying to force my legs closed was my last desperate attempt to stop him, the skin around my wrists burning as fabric cut into my flesh while I struggled against the bounds.

But it was no use. I already felt him nudging against my entrance, his heavy body keeping me pinned down.

"Don't do this," I pleaded, out of breath. "Don't."

A cold palm flattened against the side of my face, forcing my head deeper into the mattress, making sure I wasn't going anywhere.

"After this, you'll be mine in every. Fucking. Way."

The familiar burn started—the ache, the pain, the humiliation. I felt it, starting at the apex of my thighs as I felt my own brother on the verge of desecrating my body in the worst way possible.

"Jesus," he whimpered, pushing his lips against my shoulders. "I get it now. I get why all those men came back for you night after night. I'm not even inside you yet, and I could come right now."

"Oh, God." I wept, the sheets already soaked with my tears. I tried to stop him somehow, holding my breath and pushing down hard to keep him from forcing himself inside me. But all I felt was the warmth against my legs as I pissed myself while my brother's grunts started to fill my ears like devil's breaths.

In those moments, I did what he had taught me to do. I turned it off. I became nothing, a void unable to feel a thing. I was that ten-year-old girl again, only this time I didn't pray for someone to save me.

I prayed to die.

ONYX

WARM BLOOD CLUNG to my skin. Rage was pounding like a heavy metal song inside my head, my bones thundering against my flesh. Storming into the Python compound, the Kings and Sixes standing together, the way it had always been, just felt fucking right.

This was it. This was the day we'd been waiting for. The day my brother and I had been dreaming of since we watched our father take his last breath, courtesy of a Python blade.

There was no stopping us. It was war, and we were determined to win. But every time my bullets pierced flesh and the knife in my hand slit throats, all I saw was her. Her beautiful face, striking eyes, and lethal betrayal. The blade I used to kill these fuckers belonged to her. Such beautiful irony.

Even after her deceit came to light, I couldn't help but worry that she might be here, that somehow she'd be caught in the crossfire. And my head still tried to make sense of why she never told Slither about me taking Granite's place. My heart kept trying to convince my head that maybe she didn't tell him because her loyalty had shifted. Her heart had changed—for me.

A guy could hope.

"Where's Slither?" Ink yelled over the screams and grunts of pain.

"Fucker ain't here." A slimy Python came storming toward me from the front, but I saw him coming, and I jabbed my blade right into his gut, twisting the knife and feeling his warm blood gush over my hand. There wasn't time for me to relish my kill, bask in the blood of my enemy. And since these guys wore the Pythons cut, they were scum like Slither, which meant they had to die...just like him.

Crow's men circled a bunch of prospects, hacking away at them. The Sixes were our allies, but they were brutal. They were beasts, and they killed like savages—like mother-fucking Vikings with huge-ass smiles on their faces.

"Where the fuck is he?" Ink searched around, and I could see the desperation on his face, the need to find the one man he had been waiting months for.

Looking to the right, I spotted a flight of stairs. "Yo, Ink. Up there."

He nodded and rushed in that direction, and I followed. Granite, Dutch, and Manic knew how to take care of them-selves. And with Crow fighting by their side, they sure as fuck didn't need me or Ink.

Warning prickled at the back of my neck, and my instincts flared. I turned around, seeing a Python aim right at Ink's back. Launching forward, I crashed into Ink, taking him to the ground. My jaw hit the edge of the stairs, pain thundering through the side of my face. But there was no time to shake it, catching the frame of a man coming toward us. His eyes were pinned on Ink, lips pulled in a snarl as he aimed his gun. Without thinking even for a second, I grabbed my gun, aimed, and pulled the motherfucking trigger.

The guy stumbled back, staring down at his chest, eyes wide with surprise. Why, I didn't know. Fuckers around here should have known I never missed a goddamn shot.

He sagged to the ground, a corpse by the time his head hit the floor. Ink looked my way and gave a slight nod—a silent thank you between brothers.

We got up and rushed up the stairs, war still raging behind us. But Ink was like a fucking bloodhound with only one target in mind.

I was still figuring out why I was running behind him, searching. Was I looking for Slither, wanting to end his life? Or did I want to find her? Was I searching for Wraith to make sure she was okay, even if I wasn't sure about the depth of her deception? Judging by the way my heart raced, my head filled with images of her, I knew it was the latter.

"Typical. Fucking coward. Hides whenever shit goes down." Ink searched across the top floor. I was no fucking empath, but I could feel the rage ooze out of his pores. Part of me was unsure what to expect once we did find Slither. Ink's anger ran too deep, and once he got his hands on this fucktard, there would be no stopping him. But the problem was, I wanted my own pound of flesh. Truth be told, I thought every King, and now Crow as well, wanted a piece of Slither.

We ran down the hall, the noise and chaos of the war downstairs slowly disappearing into the background.

Ink stilled as he stared at all the doors. "Fucker has to be here somewhere."

I rushed up to the first door on the left. "We'll break down every fucking door if we have to." I reared back and kicked the door. Ink joined, and we had it in splinters within seconds. We broke door after door, but Slither wasn't in any of the rooms.

Sweat dripped down the side of my face, and I wiped it away with my arm. That was when my eye caught the door right at the end. "Let's try that one."

Ink and I both hurried down the corridor, adrenaline burning through my blood.

We started kicking at the door the second we reached it, desperate to get to whoever was on the other side.

The wood cracked beneath our assault, the lock breaking from the frame. The first thing I saw was her face. Cold, lifeless, completely void. And then I saw him, the monster with his inked scales, on top of her, pinning her to the bed. That was the moment everything disappeared, when I lost myself to blinding rage. There were no thoughts running through my head, no noise, no life. Just a frenzy of fury that blazed from the pit of my stomach, all the way up my chest and out my mouth, the devil's roar ripping from my throat.

Tunnel vision of crimson had me seeing nothing but blood. I didn't even fucking blink, my feet rushing forward while I only had one goal. To slaughter.

I cursed as I grabbed him, tearing him off her, clawing my fingers into his motherfucking filthy flesh.

"Get the fuck off her!" Pulling him away and slamming my fist in his face happened at the same time, without even taking a breath.

He stumbled back, and that was when I saw it—his dick hanging out of his pants. My mind split into pieces, my heart no longer beating. I glanced from him to Wraith, lying lifeless on the bed, dress torn, arms bound...legs spread open.

Jesus fucking Christ. This wasn't happening.

This wasn't fucking happening.

Everything froze. Him. Her. Ink. Me. That exact moment came to a crashing halt, everything except my thoughts.

The horror, it was too much—and I couldn't think straight, not while I was struggling to breathe.

Torn within the moment, not knowing what to do next, I stood there unable to move.

Was she alive? Was she breathing?

Did I give in to the rage and kill this motherfucker first, or did I listen to the voice echoing from deep in my soul screaming at me to go to her. To make sure she was okay.

God, she needed me. Wraith needed me.

Right then, nothing else mattered. The lies, the blood-lust, the war, the past—nothing fucking mattered. Nothing but her.

I rushed to her side. "Wraith?" With panicked breaths, I hovered over her, brushing her tangled hair from her face, revealing a busted lip and blood smears on her cheeks, a cut just above her eye. "Jesus, what did he do to you?" I untied her hands, her skin torn and raw from the bindings. "Jesus. Wraith."

I crouched, palming her cheek, willing her to wake up, desperate for her to open her eyes and let me see the color in her irises again.

"Wraith?" She didn't respond, and fear slammed against my chest, threatening to take me to the ground. "Wraith, please talk to me." Her body was cold, her face pale. I just...I couldn't think...I didn't know what the fuck to do.

"You sick motherfucker! What did you do to her?" I screamed at the top of my voice, panic and rage resonating in every word, dripping like toxins from my body. When I glanced over my shoulder, he was gone. There was no trace of him or Ink. It was like they both simply vanished, but I couldn't give a shit. I didn't care that he was gone. All I cared about was her.

Sweeping her up in my arms, I rushed out of the room and down the hall. "Stay with me, beautiful. Stay with me." My feet couldn't carry me fast enough. It felt like I wasn't moving at all, the race against time keeping me frozen in that one moment. Faster, I needed to go faster. I needed to make sure she was okay.

The second I reached the top of the stairs, I met Granite's eyes, and he immediately knew something was wrong, wasting no time to meet me halfway.

"What happened?"

"I don't know. I don't know what the fuck...Jesus," I couldn't talk. I couldn't think.

"Manic," Granite called, "get the van, and call Doc. Tell him you're on your way."

"Jesus, what...oh, God." Tears stung my eyes, panic running rampant through my body. "Wraith, wake up. Dear God. Granite, he hurt her." I fell to my knees, clutching her against my chest. "The fucker hurt her."

"Who? Who hurt her?" Granite crouched and took her wrist, feeling her pulse. "She's still alive, Onyx. Who hurt her?"

"Slither. Ink and I...we...fuck!"

"What happened? Talk, Onyx."

My hands shook as I brushed the hair from her face, wanting nothing more than for her to open her eyes. "Slither...he hurt her. Ink and I stormed into the room... and...and," I looked up, Granite staring at me with worry, "I think he raped her."

"Jesus." Granite paled. "Where is he? Where's Ink?"

I shook my head almost manically. "I don't know. I don't know where they are."

"We'll search the building." I heard Crow's voice. "We'll find them."

"Okay, come on." Granite helped me up, and I only clutched Wraith tighter against me, my entire body shaking. "Get her to Doc now. We'll finish this."

"Granite—"

"I know, brother. We'll find him. But you need to take care of her first. Make sure she's okay. Remember," he pinned his stare on mine, "she comes first. Fuck everything else."

I nodded and carried her out of there, leaving the war behind, not caring who died or who lived. Just as long as she did. Just as long as she was okay. Nothing else mattered but her.

Just her...

Just. Her.

"SHE'S GOING TO BE OKAY." Granite pulled up a chair and sat down beside me. "Doc says it's just trauma."

"She needs to wake up." I refused to take my eyes off her, leaning as close to her as possible.

"She will. Doc gave her something so she can sleep, to allow her body to shake most of the shock. We don't know what happened between her and Slither—"

I snapped my glare to him. "Are you kidding? Do you not see the bruises on her face? Did you not see what she looked like when I carried her out of the hellhole?"

"Relax, man," he held up his hand, "chill. At least we know he didn't rape her."

I took a breath, my head hanging down. It was just too disgusting and vile to even try to comprehend that her own brother would want to rape her. "What kind of sick fuck would want to rape his own sister?"

Granite shook his head. "I dunno, man. Just when I think Slither reached an all-time low."

I closed my eyes, trying to find a motherfucking silver lining before I lost my mind. At least we got there in time, and Slither was unable to desecrate her in the most horrific ways possible. God, I couldn't even think about it.

Rubbing my palms across my beard, I glanced at him. "Ink back yet?"

"Yeah."

"Did they find him?"

Granite shook his head, his expression grim and despondent.

"Fuck," I cursed. "Where the fuck did he disappear to?"

"I have no idea."

"Every time we think we have him, fucker manages to get away."

Granite rubbed the back of his neck. "I was sure tonight would be it, that we'd finally have him. And judging by the way Ink stormed in here, my guess is he thought the same."

"I would have killed him." I looked at Granite. "I would have killed the motherfucker tonight."

"I know." Granite let out a heavy breath. "Everyone wants a piece of this fucker now. Even Crow is out there searching for him, and if he gets his hands on Slither before we do, Ink will lose his shit. He's so hellbent on being the one who drives a knife through that fucker's heart."

I rubbed my palms together. "After the rage I felt tonight, I can't even imagine what Ink's feeling."

Wraith stirred and let out a subtle moan. I jumped up, standing by her side within the blink of an eye. "Wraith."

"Where," her eyes fluttered, "where am I?"

I reached out for her hand but thought better of it. After what she went through, the last thing she probably needed was another man's touch. "It's okay. You're safe."

Abruptly, she sat up in the bed. "Glenn." Her face was pale as a ghost, and I could see the vein in her neck going completely apeshit.

Granite and I looked at each other, confused.

"I mean," she shook her head lightly, "my brother. Slither." Her panicked gaze swept around the room, her chest rising and falling rapidly.

"Wraith, listen to me." This time I ignored my head and followed my heart, taking her hand in mine. "You're safe. He can't hurt you here."

Wild eyes glimmering with tears found mine. "The last thing I remember..." She choked back on her words. "Did he...did my brother—"

"No." I shook my head. "No, he didn't. We got there before he could...before he could hurt you further."

The relief that visibly flooded over her was heartbreaking to witness. The thought of her thinking her own brother had hurt her in such a way was too twisted to even comprehend.

"Where is he?" Her voice was nothing but a whisper.

"We don't know. He got away. Wraith, listen," I crouched by the side of her bed, looking up at her, clutching her hand between my palms, "I'm sorry. I'm sorry for the things I said to you, that I didn't give you a chance to explain."

There was a weary look in her eyes screaming uncertainty as she studied me. "Onyx, I'm sorry."

"What happened, Wraith? Did he blackmail you, force you to do all these things?"

I saw her hesitate before shaking her head. "He didn't blackmail me, Onyx. He didn't force me to do anything."

"Then why? I can't believe you'd do those *things* simply because you wanted to."

She grabbed the sheet and tried to get off the bed. "I have to go."

"He manipulated you."

Both Wraith and I turned toward the door, Granite

standing to the side as Neon stepped in with her crutch. "Slither manipulated you into doing these things for him, didn't he?"

Glancing from Neon to Wraith, I got the sense that Neon saw something in Wraith, something she recognized. So, I stepped back, trying to remove myself from the picture in the hopes Neon might be able to crack through the hard surface of Wraith's secrets.

Neon didn't take her eyes off Wraith, and I could see her compassion shining through. I felt it all across the room. It was like that night in the bar, when they met for the first time. There was this weird connection between them—and now, something told me that connection was Slither.

Neon took a few more steps inside the room, her lips pulled in a straight line. Her hair, which had always been some color or other of the rainbow, was now merely a faded light brown, and where she always wore heavy make-up, there was no trace of it on her face now, only the marks the cigarette burns left behind. It had been months, and even though she was recovering physically, she still wasn't the Neon they took from us that day.

Wraith's eyes were burdened with heavy tears. "I'm so sorry for what my brother did to you."

"He almost did the same to you."

I cringed at Neon's words, grinding my teeth just thinking about what that sick bastard wanted to do to his own goddamn sister.

Wraith looked down, nervously picking at her finger-nails. "I knew he was cruel, heartless." She glanced at Neon. "But he's my brother, and the only family I have left. I guess I didn't want to see the monster he has become." She inclined her head. "But now I know."

Wraith chewed on her lip as her gaze drifted from Neon,

to Granite, to me. She was weary, I could see it. Like prey trapped by a pack of hunters, unsure whether she would be spared or slaughtered.

Neon placed her crutches against the wall, hopping on one leg toward the chair. I knew better than to offer my help. She'd rather chew on wood than accept it.

"No one blames you for trusting your brother, Wraith. Everyone here knows how important family is."

Wraith simply nodded, folding her hands in her lap.

"I can see you're uncertain. You don't know who to trust anymore, which is why you want to rush out of here." Neon took a seat. "But let me tell you this. These men might look like mean motherfuckers, but behind those stone-cold expressions, filthy mouths, and muscle bags are teeny-tiny little unicorn hearts."

Granite snorted, and even among all the drama and hurt, I had to crack a smile.

Wraith snickered, and I loved the sound. It was fucking beautiful, and it woke this urge inside me to go to her and wrap my arms around her tiny frame. To just hold her, and tell her everything was fucking fine, even if I didn't know the whole truth yet.

Neon righted herself in the chair, grimacing a little. "Listen, pretty, Slither is one fucked up individual. I know he's your brother and all, but that man," Neon's expression turned to pure hatred, "that man isn't human. To say he's a monster would be a fucking compliment to whatever the fuck he really is. But here's the thing." She leaned forward, and everyone could see how fucking serious she was. "When I look at you, I don't see him. I don't see the same evil in your eyes. He's disgusting, vile, and absolutely revolting—an immoral fucker who probably won't burn in hell one day, but rather rule alongside the fucking devil. But you," she shook her head, "you ain't the same. You ain't him. And even though he's your brother, something tells me there's more to it."

Heavy silence draped over all of us, the atmosphere in the room palpable as we all waited in anticipation for Wraith to tell the truth, to tell us why she did Slither's bidding. I prayed to God it wasn't merely simple sibling loyalty. To think she was his rat only because she wanted to be was insane. It was something I couldn't comprehend since I couldn't wrap my head around it, and there was nothing more disgraceful than a motherfucking rat.

Wraith cleared her throat, the bruise on her jaw growing more prominent by the minute, the blue and black colors a stark contrast against her pale white skin.

"Our mom, she was hooked on heroin." Her throat bobbed as she swallowed. "The only way she could afford her dirty habit was to..." she closed her eyes, her expression pained, and my chest ached for her, "...the only way they could get the money was to have some of our dad's friends use us—" She choked on her tears.

"Jesus," I cursed.

"How old were you?" Neon urged her to continue.

"Ten."

"Jesus fucking Christ!" I wanted to slam my fist into the wall, break fucking skin. It was too much. Ten years old? What the fuck?

Rage erupted, searing the inside of my veins. With my fists balled and my blood smothered with anger, I was on the verge of starting fucking Armageddon in this goddamn city.

Granite shot me a knowing look, a subtle way of telling me to keep my shit together—for Wraith's sake. So, I bit my tongue and clenched my jaw. The last thing Wraith needed was to see me lose control.

"Did they rape him too? Slither?" Neon kept pushing for more, like she wanted Wraith to let it all out. Meanwhile, I was standing there feeling sick to my motherfucking stomach.

"Yes," Wraith mumbled softly. "They hurt both of us."

I scoffed. Somehow, the idea of Slither being hurt as well settled my rage a little. I knew he was young and innocent back then, but not even that reality was able to make me hate him less.

"For how long?" Neon asked.

Wraith pressed her lips together before answering, "Five years. It continued for five years." Wraith blinked, her eyes red and moist as she looked in my direction. "Until he killed them."

I straightened. "Who?"

"Slither...he killed our parents."

That was when a puzzle piece slid into place. "At the beach, you said your brother took care of whoever it was that hurt you. You were talking about Slither killing your parents."

She simply nodded, her shoulders slumped forward, tears falling from her cheeks and onto her lap. With the back of her hand, she wiped at her face. "Slither joined a biker crew, made some friends in pretty dark places. On the night of my fifteenth birthday, he brought some friends home, and it all ended."

"He killed them?"

Wraith nodded. "He killed them and burned their bodies along with the house."

"And that's why you were loyal to him," Neon stated.

"You felt like you owed him because he made the abuse stop. The rape. The torture."

This time, sobs wracked through her body, her shoulders shuddering as sorrow tore her apart. Her cries were gut-wrenching, and it grated against my spine causing me physical fucking pain. I couldn't take it anymore, seeing her like this. Witnessing her agony. It was just too fucking much.

I rushed over to her, taking her face in my hands and forcing her to look at me. "I'm sorry."

"No, you don't have to—"

"I'm sorry, Wraith. I'm sorry for what your parents did to you. I'm sorry for what your brother did to you. And by God," I inhaled sharply, "I'm sorry for what I said to you."

She placed her hands over mine, her tears telling tales of too many sorrows for one person to carry. "I'm sorry I hurt you."

"No." I shook my head almost violently, biting my bottom lip. "Don't you dare say you're sorry. Don't you ever fucking apologize, you hear me? Ever."

I kissed her. I took her mouth with mine, and I tried my damnedest to kiss away every ounce of pain this woman carried around inside her. She was no fucking void. She wasn't a wraith. Her life would have been so much better had she been empty like her name implied. Her soul was filled to the brim with so much hurt, as everyone who was supposed to protect her didn't. Those who were supposed to keep her safe were the ones who put her in harm's way. Well, not anymore.

My lips remained on hers for a while longer, and I could taste her sorrow as her tears penetrated our kiss. Placing my head against hers, I weaved my hand in her hair. "I swear to fucking God, no one will ever hurt you again."

Her sobs cracked, hiccupped as she cried. "Onyx—"

"I'm in love with you, Wraith. And I think I've been in love with you since you sat down at my goddamn table, pretending to be my date."

She let out a half-hearted laugh, a beautiful sound that fused with her sorrow.

"I don't care who you are, whose blood runs through your veins, I will take care of you. No one will ever touch you again but me."

I sucked in a breath when I felt her wrap her arms around my neck, pulling me closer, crying as she buried her face into my neck. "I didn't think I'd ever be able to love someone," she whispered between tears. "But now, because of you, I know I can."

From the corner of my eye, I saw Neon standing by the door about to walk out. There was a gentle smile on her face, and I knew she pushed Wraith to tell the truth so I could realize exactly how much this fucking woman meant to me. No lies, no amount of betrayal, no crew, no rules, and no motherfucking president tag would ever change that.

"Wraith," I took her chin in my fingers, gently lifting her face to mine, "I want you to stay with me. I want you to be with me, be my woman."

She nodded, face wet with lingering tears.

"But you need to know, I'm going to search for him. I'm going to turn this motherfucking city upside down, and I will find him. And when I do," I tightened my grip on her chin a little, gritting my teeth, "I'm going to kill him. You understand that? I am going to kill...your brother."

For the longest time, she just stared back at me, not saying a single word. Her striking blue eyes were faded, tired, red from purging herself of so much pain and sorrow. Yet as she placed a palm against my cheek, some of the blue hues in her irises illuminated. "I know you need to do what needs to be done."

I was probably being a beast for smiling at her words, but I couldn't help it. Her words showed her strength, proved there was still iron left in her will to live, in her drive to take back what had been taken from her.

I was no idiot. I knew this was only the beginning of our road to happiness, and that we probably had to get to know one another again since all of this started with a lie. But what I did know was I was never letting her go, no matter what. I finally understood how and why Granite made the decisions he did once Alyx came into his life. Love changed a man. It made you realize what was important, what really fucking mattered.

Family and love mattered, nothing else.

I was the president of the American Street Kings, and I would do whatever I had to in order to protect my brothers, our women, our family.

And no one would be able to stop me.

EPILOGUE

INK

IT SMELLED like dead rodent in here, and I could practically feel the filth cling to my skin. It was warm, humid, the summer heat surrounding us like a motherfucking bitch, and the lack of ventilation made it a thousand times worse.

I walked across the concrete floor, my heavy footsteps echoing with menace. The way my heart raced, adrenaline and excitement brewing in my gut, I could feel my blood sing with vengeance.

The constant drip of water was annoying as fuck. *Drip, drip, drip.* I imagined the water dripping in a pool of blood, the crimson spreading through the ripples. Blood, it was all I thought about.

Blood. Death. Pain. So much fucking pain.

The day we found Neon's mutilated body on the pavement, dropped there like she was nothing but a sack of garbage, something inside me died. I flipped a motherfucking switch, and now the hate was controlling me. I couldn't even sleep without dreaming about her, about him, how he hurt her, tortured her, leaving nothing beautiful untouched. Every thought I'd had since that day was soaked in hate and rage, my need for revenge making it worse as seconds, minutes, days, weeks passed by without coming close to sating the bloodlust.

Neon had grown stronger, physically. But everyone knew her mind was still stuck in that room—the room where they destroyed her. She was no longer the carefree woman who walked around infecting everyone with her laughter, causing everyone to love her without even trying. Her light was everywhere, and I had been drawn to it since the first day I met her. There was this part of me that always wanted to be close to her, but I stopped myself from getting too close. I was too afraid my darkness would taint her light. I didn't want to ruin the good in her, and acting like an asshole was the only way to keep the walls up around my heart. I knew I could never make her mine. She was too good for a manwhore like me. Her soul was too beautiful for the ugliness I carried in me. But there were days I found it half impossible not to act on my feelings for her, days when I made snarky remarks, remarks everyone laughed about. Remarks everyone thought were mere jokes, little acts of assholery. Eventually, it became our *thing*, the bickering, the banter. God, I lived for the fucking banter between us. It was my way of allowing myself a sliver of her light—a second in time when I pretended I was worthy of her.

The day Slither took her from us—from me—my ugliness turned into something menacing and grotesque. Yet the walls around my heart came tumbling down, falling into a heap of dust. Now, I was determined to make her mine. It was crazy, insane, stupid, but during those hours when I believed I had lost her, all I thought about was how I wished I had acted like the selfish asshole everyone knew I was and allowed myself to be with her like I longed to. I would have rather had her for a moment than never at all. So, when we found her, however fucked up, I decided right there and then I would never, ever fucking stop until I'd made her mine. I would fight for her until the day I took my last breath. She would be mine...someday. But first, I had a promise to keep. The day I picked her beaten-up, half-dead body from the pavement, carrying her inside, I swore to her I would make this right for her. I vowed to make her tormenter pay with every last drop of his blood. I would never stop until I'd avenged her pain.

I leaned against the plastered wall, lighting a cigarette, feeling how the smoke stuck to my throat as it went down to settle in my lungs.

Slither always managed to escape us somehow, finding a way to mind-fuck us while he skidded his evil ass out of every situation where we thought we had him. He was like the motherfucking Houdini of street crews. I was starting to lose my patience, the itch for retaliation becoming like a virus. Deep down, I knew Onyx and Granite made the best decisions for the crew. I respected them for it. But my promise to Neon was something I was hellbent on keeping, no matter what.

No. Matter. What.

When Onyx and I rushed into that room, catching Slither with his dick out of his pants, Wraith lying on the bed like dead prey, I knew we had him. But with Onyx caught in a freak-out frenzy, I knew Slither would not live long enough to see another day. There was a bullet in Onyx's gun with Slither's name on, and it would have been lodged in his skull before dawn. Onyx's anger would have taken away my chance to fulfill my promise to Neon, and I couldn't let that happen.

Taking a few more deep drags, I exhaled a cloud of smoke before flicking the bud to the floor and stomping on it then making my way down the dark corridor. The only light came from the room right at the end—the same room where they tortured and raped Neon for hours. The closer I got to the light, the more I felt wickedness stir in me, a malevolent justice knocking at my skull. Every inch of my skin prickled with the rush of adrenaline, an exhilarating restlessness gnawing at my bones.

I stepped into the room, my black boots a stark contrast against the white tiles, perfect to see every drop of blood I would spill.

Pulling out the knife in my pocket, I looked up and smiled, the sight before me making my blood sing with victory. "Welcome to my world, snake. Are you ready to shed some skin?"

~

The series continues in...

DESTROYED.

OTHER NOVELS BY BELLA J

The Twisted Duet
Blood and Lies (Twisted Duet, Book 1)
Blood and Vows (Twisted Duet, Book 2)

The Royal Mafia Series
Mafia Princess (Royal Mafia, Book 1)
Mafia Prince (Royal Mafia, Book 2)
Mafia King (Royal Mafia, Book 3)
Mafia Queen (Royal Mafia, Book 4)

The Shattered Secrets Duet
Regret (Shattered Secrets, Book 1)
Torment (Shattered Secrets, Book 2)

The Resplendence Series
Ruin (Resplendence, Book 1)
Rush (Resplendence, Book 2)
Rage (Resplendence, Book 3)

ABOUT THE AUTHOR

All the way from Cape Town, South Africa, Bella J lives for the days when she's able to retreat to her writer's cave where she can get lost in her little pretend world of romance, love, and insanely hot bad boys.

Bella J is a Hybrid Author with both Self-Published and Traditional Published work. Even though her novels range from drama, to comedy, to suspense, it's the dark, twisted side of romance she loves the most.